RETURN of the
EMERALD SKULL

PAUL STEWART & CHRIS RIDDELL

Barnaby Grimes

RETURN of the EMERALD SKULL

Illustrated by Chris Riddell

d|b
David Fickling Books
OXFORD · NEW YORK

A DAVID FICKLING BOOK

Published by David Fickling Books
an imprint of Random House Children's Books
a division of Random House, Inc.
New York

Originally published in Great Britain by David Fickling Books,
an imprint of Random House Children's Books, in 2008.

David Fickling Books and colophon are trademarks of David Fickling.

Visit us on the Web!
www.randomhouse.com/kids

Educators and librarians, for a variety of teaching tools, visit us at
www.randomhouse.com/teachers

Library of Congress Cataloging-in-Publication Data is available upon request.

ISBN 978-0-385-75128-5 (trade)—ISBN 978-0-385-75129-2 (lib. bdg.)—
ISBN 978-0-375-89169-4 (e-book)

Printed in the United States of America
February 2009
10 9 8 7 6 5 4 3 2 1
First American Edition

For Anna, Katy and Jack

CHAPTER 1

'*C*ut out his beating heart!' the ancient voice commanded, each syllable dripping with a dark evil that I was powerless to resist.

Overhead, the moon slid slowly but inexorably across the face of the sun, casting the courtyard into a dreadful dusk. And as the light faded, so did the last vestiges of my will to resist. There was nothing I could do.

A circle of shadowy figures clustered like a flock of hideous vultures around the great slab that lay before me. Their beaked faces and long rustling feathers quivered with awful anticipation as their dark eye-sockets turned, as one, towards me.

On awkward, stumbling legs I approached the wooden altar like a sleepwalker, climbing one step after the other, powerless to fight it.

The hideous figures parted as I drew closer. At the altar I looked down. There, stripped to the waist, lying face up and spread-eagled, was a man, roped into place. There were cuts and weals on his skin – some scabbed over, some fresh – and his ribs were sticking up, giving his chest the appearance of a damaged glockenspiel.

His head lolled to one side, and from his parted lips there came a low, rasping moan.

'Please,' he pleaded, gazing up at me with the panic-stricken eyes of a ferret-cornered rabbit. 'Don't do it, I'm begging you . . .'

At that moment the final dazzling rays of the sun were extinguished by the dark orb of the moon. In shock, I looked up into the sky. The whole disc had turned pitch-black, and from the circumference of the circle a spiky ring of light streamed out in all directions, like a black merciless eye staring down from the heavens.

The tallest of the feathered figures stepped forward to face me. He wore a great crown of iridescent blue plumage. Behind him, nestling like a grotesque egg on the cushion of a high-backed leather chair, was a hideous grinning skull. As I stared, the huge jewels in the skull's eye-sockets started to glow a bright and bloody crimson, which stained the eerie twilight of the eclipse.

The feathered figure reached into his cape and withdrew a large stone knife, which he held out to me. Again the ancient voice rasped in my head.

'Cut out his beating heart!'

Despite myself, I reached out and gripped the haft of the stone knife in my hands. As I did so, I felt my arm being raised up into the air, as if it was attached to a string tugged upwards by some unseen puppeteer.

The feathered figure reached into his cape and withdrew a large stone knife . . .

I stared down at the figure tied to the altar. A vivid cross of red paint marked the spot beneath which his heart lay, beating, I was sure, as violently as my own.

My grip tightened on the cruel stone knife, the blade glinting, as the blood-red ruby eyes of the grinning skull bored into mine. Inside my head, the voice rose to a piercing scream.

'Cut out his beating heart – and give it to me!'

CHAPTER
2

*H*ow could I have possibly known of
the waking nightmare that was to
unfold when, on a bright summer afternoon,
I set off for Grassington Hall School with a
spring in my step and a whistle on my lips?

I don't know about you, but schools have
always struck me as strange, unnatural institutions. Don't get me wrong: I'm certainly
not against hard study and the acquiring of
knowledge. Far from it! Why, there's nothing
I like better than poring over the dusty
volumes on the shelves of Underhill's Library
for Scholars of the Arcane after a hard day's
work . . .

I'm a tick-tock lad by profession – that's a clerk errant for those of you who might not know. I pick up things and deliver them all over this great city as quickly as I can manage, because – tick-tock – time is money!

The faster I am, the more I earn. Simple as that.

That's the reason I always take the most direct route from one place to another, over the rooftops. Highstacking, it's called, and it's not for the faint-hearted, I can tell you. I've taken my fair share of tumbles in my time. It goes with the job, and it's one of the reasons there aren't more highstackers around. It's just too dangerous for most tick-tock lads, who prefer to stick to the pavements. 'Cobblestone-creepers', we highstackers call them. Needs practice, daring and a sense of adventure to take to the rooftops, not to mention an instinct for danger.

Now, *that's* something they don't teach

you at those fancy schools.

Instead, the pampered sons and daughters of the rich are packed off to grand-sounding institutions like Highfield Academy for Young Ladies of Quality and Farrow Court College for the Sons of the Gentry, where they're taught to dance and ride to hounds and hold polite conversations in whatever language is considered fashionable at that moment.

Not that all schools are as grand as Highfield and Farrow. No, I've seen my fair share of institutions that resemble lunatic asylums or prisons rather than places of learning. Set up by plausible professors with impressive-sounding letters after their names, these schools promise to make ladies and gentlemen out of their unfortunate students and charge gullible parents exorbitant fees to match.

'Lock-up academies', they're called, because once they're full, the professors lock the gates and control everything that comes in or out. That way they can pocket the fees and not spend so much as a brass farthing on their pupils.

Old Jenkins the cloth merchant pays little Johnny's school fees, and in return gets a letter each term from the apple of his eye telling him how splendidly he's getting on. The truth, though, is quite different. Little Johnny and his schoolmates are being starved and beaten, and sleeping ten to a vermin-infested bed, while Professor Whackstick and his schoolmaster henchmen get richer and richer.

I know, believe me, because as a tick-tock lad I've delivered a good few sackfuls of 'school letters'. Whenever I discover they're fake or have been written under threat, I do my best to warn the parents – but it's amazing how often they'd rather not know. Besides, what's the word of a tick-tock lad against that of a plausible professor?

No wonder, then, that there are school rebellions.

Yes, that's right. Rebellions. When the poor downtrodden inmates of the lock-up academies just can't stand it any more.

Take Grendel Grange School, for instance. The pupils spent months fashioning all manner of weapons right under the noses of the bullying headmaster, Colonel Griggs, and his staff of ex-military men, who were supposed to be giving their charges the 'discipline and moral fibre of a military education'. The good colonel certainly got more than he bargained for.

Despite being fed on rations of mouldy bread and watery gruel, the Grendel Grange Grenadiers – as they called themselves – managed to rout the teachers in a pitched battle and besiege them in the Senior Common Room for five days, using catapults, blowpipes and a home-made cannon.

Of course, the most famous school rebellion took place a few years earlier, at Enderby Court College for Young Ladies. The Enderby Amazons defeated Dame Cecily Mandrake and her fifty-strong staff of ex-convicts using croquet mallets and feral cats, and released the girls of the lower school, who counted the daughters of several prominent merchants and the Lord Mayor's niece amongst their number. I must confess, I played a small part in the rebellion, due to my close friendship with one Emily Ford-Maddox, a girl with startling green eyes and a pretty smile . . .

But that's another story.

As I say, schools vary. There are good ones like Highfield Academy and Farrow, and shockingly bad ones like Grendel Grange and Enderby Court. Grassington Hall was, by the standards of the day, a good school. It was situated to the south of the city, where the mills and factories give way to parkland

and meadows; where cobbles end and grassy lanes begin. It's possible, out there, to imagine yourself in the country as you walk past the spacious villas with their large gardens and ornamental lakes. Once, late one summer a few years back, I even took a haywain ride at midnight through the southern suburbs during the terrifying scarecrow zombie scare . . .

Anyway, the gardens were in full bloom and the birds were singing in the hedgerows as I approached the entrance to Grassington Hall on that bright summer afternoon. I arrived at the gatehouse, which was set into a high perimeter wall at the end of the drive, with an urgent delivery for the headmaster, one Archimedes Barnett, BA (Hons), MA, MRSA.

There were boys out on the field playing 'Farrow Fives' – a game invented originally at Farrow Court, and very popular at the time. It was, as far as I could tell, a cross between baseball and croquet, and involved hitting five large targets situated in the outfield. Whatever the rules, it also involved a lot of running and shouting, by the look of it, not to mention a fair few crunching tackles.

I explained my business to the gatekeeper, a cheerful-looking fellow of middling years, with a waxed moustache and a warm hand-shake. I'd seen his type before. An ex-soldier, by the look of his upright bearing and neatly trimmed side-whiskers. Probably a private in the infantry – though the boys all called him 'the Major'. He summoned one of the lads to take me to the headmaster's study.

'Thompson, here, will show you the way,' he told me, indicating the fair-haired lad in a scruffy white blazer and grey, grass-stained knee breeches. 'Mr Barnett will be mighty pleased to see you. That's if he *can* see you,' he added with a chuckle. 'Right now, he's as blind as a corporal in a coal cellar.'

Thompson, my guide, seemed amiable enough. We took a footpath which ran parallel to the main drive, then crossed a gravelled area for visiting coaches and carriages. The walls of the buildings were made of local stone – a pale grey colour, where they weren't covered with dense ivy. We went through an archway and across a large quadrangle with an ornate fountain, then through a second grander archway on the other side, which led into the main building – a magnificent, echoing structure with lots of glazed tiles and dark wood.

As we entered, I noticed the pupils we met looked healthy and well cared for, smiling and doffing their white tasselled caps politely as we passed.

This clearly was no 'lock-up academy', I thought as we headed for the stairs.

The sweeping staircase was as grand as everything else I had seen, the walls lined with portraits. We emerged onto a landing and turned right towards the east wing. Moments later, Thompson stopped in front of a broad oak door, the slightly tarnished plaque informing me that we had arrived at our destination.

'Here we are, sir,' he said. 'The headmaster's study. Would you like me to introduce you, sir?'

'No, no,' I said. 'I can do that myself. You go back to your game ... And thank you,' I added as he turned and strode back down the corridor.

I knocked on the door.

'Enter,' came a thin, reedy-sounding voice.

I did so. The room was simply decorated. There was an ornate but worn rug on the floor; there were large bookcases to the right and two leaded windows to the left, in front of which stood a broad desk, the wood as dark as ebony. An elderly, white-haired gentleman who I took to be the headmaster,

Archimedes Barnett, was stooped over a letter he was writing, his face so close to the desktop that his nose was all but grazing the vellum. As I approached the desk, he looked up and squinted at me though narrowed eyes, his brow creased with concentration.

'Yes, boy? What can I do for you?' he said, the quill poised in his right hand. 'Speak up, I haven't got all day.'

'My name's Grimes, sir,' I began.

'Grimes? Grimes?' repeated the head-master, screwing up his eyes and peering at me. 'You must be a new boy ... Anyway, I hope this is important, Grimes, because I'm expecting a delivery any moment. Speak up, lad.'

'I'm not at the school, sir,' I said. 'I've been sent here by Laurence Oliphant. The opti-cian.' I reached into the fourth pocket of my poacher's waistcoat and removed a small hinged box. 'Sir, I believe this is the delivery you've been expecting.'

'It is?' the headmaster exclaimed. 'Oh, that's simply marvellous!'

I placed the box in his outstretched hand and watched as he fumbled with the lid for a moment, before opening it, removing the spectacles and slipping them on. They were steel-rimmed, with two sets of half-moon lenses, clamped together to make two circles. He pushed them up onto the bridge of his nose and blinked at me.

'Oh! That's wonderful!' he cried out. 'Absolutely wonderful!' He looked down at the letter he had been writing. 'I can see close up and' – he glanced across at yours truly, a great grin spreading from ear to ear – 'and I can see that you are not a pupil, but a clerk errant – and a fine one at that! Mr . . .'

'Grimes,' I reminded him. 'Barnaby Grimes.'

He climbed to his feet and extended a hand in greeting. I took it and shook it warmly.

'Barnaby Grimes!' he chuckled. 'Very

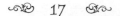

pleased to make your acquaintance, young man.'

He picked up the letter again and examined it closely, then, laying it aside, looked all round the room.

'Oh, these are far better than the ones I broke!' he said. 'That Mr Oliphant is a genius with lenses. He told me he'd get them to me at the end of school today, and here you are, Mr Grimes, and it is barely lunch time. What efficiency!'

He paused for a moment, took off the spectacles and polished them thoughtfully with a large white handkerchief, before putting them back on.

'I don't suppose,' said the headmaster, 'that I could prevail upon you, as a tick-tock lad, to accept a commission from me, Mr Grimes? You see, the problem is,' he continued, motioning for me to sit down, 'I'm just too busy to leave the school during term time, yet I have, from time to time, crates and packages that need to be picked up from the docks and brought to me. Very delicate items that have to be handled with the utmost care . . .'

I nodded, wondering what exactly these crates and packages might contain.

'But in my experience,' he went on, 'when I have employed others to run this errand for me, they've proved unsatisfactory.' He shook his head sadly. 'They drop the boxes; they manhandle them and leave them upside down. They give no thought to the contents and how delicate they might be.' He smiled. 'Unlike you, Mr Grimes. After all, you have just delivered a fragile pair of spectacles in perfect condition. If you could do the same for my little . . . packages, I would be indebted to you.'

'I'd be happy to accept, Headmaster. But these packages . . .' I said. 'Just how delicate *are* their contents?'

Mr Barnett leaned forward and touched

me lightly on the arm. 'If you'll follow me,' he said, 'I'll show you.'

The headmaster led me from his office, back along the corridor, and up to the second storey.

'No boys are allowed up here unsupervised,' he told me as he strode down to the end of a long hallway, a plush oriental rug running along its length. He stopped before a tall, heavy door with the word PRIVATE upon it, and seized the handle. 'After you, Mr Grimes,' he said, opening the door with a flourish and ushering me inside.

The chamber that lay beyond the door was long and narrow, with a high, arched ceiling, and led to a pair of tall windows at the far end. Rays of sunlight were streaming in at an angle, filling the room with a curiously rich golden light. And lining the walls – turning the already narrow room into something that was little more than an aisle – were glass display cabinets. Dozens of them. Lined up, one after the other, they towered far above my head as I walked along between them, glancing at their brightly coloured contents.

Birds.

Hundreds upon hundreds of birds. Each one lovingly stuffed and mounted in a naturalistic setting of bushes or trees, rocks or sandy scrub. Some were perching, their feet gripping branches and twigs; others were caught in flight, wings open and suspended from invisible wires.

Each of the cabinets bore a label – neatly written in black italic letters and affixed to the cabinet – which detailed the name and place of origin of the individual birds. Big birds, small birds. Male and female birds. Desert and jungle birds; birds that lived on the ocean. Small, inconspicuous birds, and large exotic birds with crests and spurs and dazzling plumage.

There were parakeets and lorikeets, and

huge multi-coloured macaws. There were giant shaggy ostriches and tiny iridescent hummingbirds. There were elegant flamingos with coral-pink feathers; storks and cranes and wild-feathered secretary birds. There were waders and warblers, dippers and divers, and peacocks in full display. There were swans, gulls and doves of every description; eagles and vultures . . .

And all of them – each and every one – were as dead as lead-peppered ducks!

The headmaster saw the expression on my face and must have interpreted it as appreciative amazement, for he smiled delightedly.

In fact, the sight of so many beautiful creatures trapped and killed in order to be preserved behind glass appalled me. But I was a tick-tock lad, and my opinion of the headmaster's little hobby was neither here nor there. If he needed someone to pick up his precious parakeets and deliver them safely, then I was the one for the job.

'Beautiful, are they not?' Archimedes Barnett beamed.

'Beautiful, are they not?' Archimedes Barnett beamed.

I nodded.

'But delicate, Mr Grimes, as I'm sure you now appreciate,' he said, gathering his thoughts. 'Bird collecting, as you can see, consumes me, body and soul. I am constantly adding to my collection, with birds being sent to me from my contacts all over the world. If you – as a tick-tock lad – could see your way to picking up these birds from the docks and bringing them safely back here to the school, I would be eternally grateful. And, of course, I should pay you most handsomely for your services.'

It seemed that these stuffed birds of his were even more important to him than the pupils in his charge. Still, it took all sorts. And anyway, who was I to judge?

'Thank you, Headmaster,' I said. 'You can rest assured, not a feather on their delicate heads shall be ruffled.'

It was obviously what the headmaster wanted to hear, for he beamed back. 'It is agreed then,' he said. 'This is most fortuitous, Mr Grimes, for I have a shipment arriving next week – a most unusual-sounding specimen, I'm sure you'll agree . . .'

'Yes?' I said, intrigued.

'The catincatapetl,' said the headmaster, 'which, translated from the ancient Toltec, means' – he paused, a dreamy smile playing across his mouth – '*the emerald messenger of darkness.*'

CHAPTER 3

A week later, I carried out the instructions the headmaster had given me. It was a Tuesday and I'd spent the morning doing my usual rounds – collecting receipts, delivering dockets, transferring forms safely from one address to another; highstacking over the sooty rooftops with hardly time to draw breath.

I set off after a spot of lunch: bread, cheese and an apple, which I ate while sitting on top of the dome of the Law Courts, leaning back against the golden statue of Justice, with her sword in one hand and scales in the other – scales which contained an apple core by the time I'd finished. It was once more a bright sunny day, though with a crisp wind coming in from the east. The blanket of smoke which hovered constantly over the poorer areas of the city was, for once, being blown across the more wealthy quarters to the west.

I headed against the wind, to an area called Riverhythe, a strip of wharves and warehouses between the East Batavia Trading Company's timberyards and the squat Spruton Bill lighthouse, built to keep the incoming and outgoing vessels from running aground on the mudflats.

In the space of twelve short years Riverhythe had been transformed from a small fisherman's rest, where fishing boats would land their catches, into a great bustling port, its jetties packed with merchant ships, cargo boats, tea clippers and dhows from the four corners of the earth. The fishmarkets and riverside shops had given way to vast warehouses and stockyards, while the water in the river itself, once sparkling, clear and teeming with fish, was now filthy, brown and utterly dead.

Yet I loved the place. I always had.

As a youngster I'd come here often to watch the ships docking to unload their cargoes and take on new ones. With its broad quays, huge jetties and great warehouses, the place was endlessly fascinating. I would sit for hours at the end of a creaking wooden jetty, just watching the endless comings and goings.

The arrival of the coal barges, for instance, was greeted by gangs of men in dirty smocks and women with baskets, who would ferry them to shore. Vast vessels, teeming with mariners and merchant seamen, would come and go, mooring side by side, the insistent cries of the dock-chiefs accompanying their movements. Clippers and cargo ships swarmed with stevedores, who shifted wares onto the barges and rowing boats moored alongside and transported them to quays and wharves further upstream. Tall, spindly cranes would load and unload the ships, great packages of merchandise swinging precariously through the air on knotted ropes to the accompaniment of yet more bellowed shouts and commands.

Every so often, with a crack and a sigh, one of the ropes would break and the crate tumble to the dock below. There it would split open and spill its wares across the ground. Then, appearing out of nowhere like a colony of ants, women and children would scamper round, grabbing whatever they could find – be it mangoes or mantillas; buttons, books, boots or bolts of cotton cloth – secrete them inside the voluminous tattered rags they wore for the purpose, and scurry away.

As I arrived that day, I saw the great stone eagle which stood atop the East Batavia Trading Company's main warehouse. That, at least, had remained. As for the rest, well, few things survived from the days of my childhood. The untidy jumble of fishermen's cottages had given way to huge fortress-like structures with iron gates and tall brick walls, while the river itself had been tamed and transformed, the mudflats largely drained and vast artificial lagoons created.

And ships! There were hundreds of them, packed into every spare inch. Barques and barges, wherries, ferries and tugs; while the biggest of them – the great clippers and traders – were so much larger than they had been in my childhood. These behemoths sported exotic names: the *Queen Mahavashti*; the *Golden Macaranda*; the *Transatalanta*. And my favourite, the *Pasacuda Princess* – a vast coal- and sail-driven vessel, sweet with the scent of the crates of exotic spices she transported from the distant islands of the Maccabees, far away in the eastern oceans.

I walked along the wharf, taking in the sights, sounds and smells, looking for the vessel the headmaster had told me would be berthed and unloading its cargo. The *Ipanema* was its name, a twin-masted schooner out of Valdario, carrying a cargo of teak and coconut oil. Not that that was of any interest to the headmaster.

No, my instructions were to find the captain, who had a carefully crated specimen with Archimedes Barnett's name on it. Judging by the banknote I had in the third pocket of my poacher's waistcoat, this Captain Luis Fernandez was going to be paid handsomely for his trouble.

'Catincatapetl,' I mused as I passed a couple of large steam tugs called *Gargantua* and *Pantagruel*.

The word had barely passed my lips when the air seemed to turn icy and the sky cloud over. I peered across the harbour to see a great bank of fog rolling up the river, like an unfurling grey carpet.

In moments, the warehouses and wharves of Riverhythe were swathed in a dense yellow mist. These sudden sea fogs – or 'fish stews', as they were called – were nothing new. Combining with the smoke from factory chimneys and thousands of domestic chimney stacks, they could be particularly thick and acrid on the dockside.

As a tick-tock lad, I hated 'fish stews'. Even the most familiar trips became fraught with uncertainty when the fog was bad. One missed turning, one forgotten landmark, and the unwary traveller was lost in an instant and, once off the beaten track, could easily fall prey to thugs, thieves and pickpockets. What was worse, their cries for help – like the calls of the market sellers, the shouts of the carriage drivers, and the howls and yowls of the dogs and cats – were so muffled that no one ever heard them.

No, when the fog descended, the city became harsh and forbidding; a place of dark secrets, darker whispers and the sound of footsteps forever fading away. Even up on the rooftops, the dense pall of stinking fog did not release its grip. And with each step a challenge and every journey a gamble, high-stacking was all but impossible, even for an expert tick-tock lad like yours truly.

Sometimes, though, far up at the top of the highest towers and steeples, the air would abruptly clear. And then, from those lofty vantage points, the yellow fog could be seen below, shifting and rolling like a filthy ocean, while sticking out of it all around – like the masts of grounded sail boats – were the tops of other buildings, each one acting as a landmark.

But down on the dockside I stood no chance. Pulling up my collar and pulling down my coalstack hat, I made my way care-fully along the wooden boardwalk, tapping with my swordstick as I went.

A little way on I stopped next to a huge tea clipper, the *Oceania*. There were lights on the deck, fuzzy with the fog but bright

enough for me to see half a dozen or so crew members in silhouette, going about their business.

'The *Ipanema*! I'm looking for the *Ipanema*!' I shouted up to an old seaman in a waxed sou'wester.

'Three vessels along, mate. You can't miss her!' he replied with a cheery wave.

'Thanks!' I shouted back, and tapped my way past.

The fog was now so thick I found it difficult to see my own hand in front of my face, let alone read the names of the dark shapes I took to be ships ahead of me.

One, two . . . three, I counted, approaching a looming black bow.

'*Ipanema* . . .' A strange, disembodied voice – half cry, half whisper – sounded close to my ear.

I paused, a shiver of apprehension running down my spine. 'Who's there?' I called into the swirling fog.

There was no reply. Gripping my sword-stick, I approached the shadowy vessel and, by tapping the boards, found the edge of the boardwalk and the beginning of a gangplank. Carefully I climbed the swaying board and stepped onto an eerie, deserted deck.

'Hello?' I called into the muffling blanket of fog. 'Is there anybody there?'

I made my way cautiously up onto the quarterdeck, and was about to push open the door to an unlit cabin when a figure loomed up at me out of the fog. I found myself staring into a pair of dead-looking eyes. In the gloom, I could just make out the tattered brocade on a brass-buttoned seaman's frock coat, and a battered cap with an ornate embroidered 'I' on its band.

'Captain?' I asked.

As if in answer, the figure thrust a small wooden crate, the size of a hatbox, into my hands. As I took it, I felt, with a flinch, the captain's ice-cold fingers brush mine.

I found myself staring into a pair of dead-looking eyes.

My fingers trembling, I fumbled with the pocket of my waistcoat for the banknote that the headmaster had given me, when the figure lurched back into the swirling mist and seemingly vanished.

By now I was thoroughly spooked – not to mention chilled to the bone and shivering like a plucked goose. I took out the note and, crouching down, found a cargo hook lying at my feet. Grasping the hook, I pinned the note to the cabin door and made a rapid exit.

Without looking back, my heart still hammering in my chest, I set off back along the boardwalk, the crate clamped firmly beneath one arm. As I did so, the fog seemed to clear as abruptly as it had rolled in, and by the time I reached the *Oceania*, daylight was breaking through the thinning mist. Glancing back over my shoulder to get a better look at the ghostly vessel I had just left, I ran slap-bang into the old seaman in the sou'wester.

'Whoa! Steady there, son!' he exclaimed, regaining his balance and catching the box that had tumbled from my hands.

He handed it back to me as I apologized for my clumsiness and hurried on my way.

It was only when I had left the docks far behind, the crate stowed securely in the haversack which hung from my shoulder, that I paused on top of a roof-ridge and caught my breath.

In the distance, the sun shone out of a blue sky down onto the masts crowded into the wharves of Riverhythe. Just beyond them, floating down the river, was the dark shape of a twin-masted schooner. I felt an icy shiver at the sight – and, glancing down, saw that the palm of my right hand was sticky with blood.

CHAPTER
4

aybe it was the cold fog that had chilled me to the marrow. Maybe it was the sinister ship with its haunted-looking captain that had thoroughly spooked me. Or maybe it was the sight of my hand, stained with someone else's blood, that had shocked me to the core. Whatever it was, highstacking it from the Riverhythe docks to Grassington Hall late that afternoon proved far from easy.

I slipped on an easy drainpipe ascent, grazing my knuckles and making a hole in the knee of my breeches. I stumbled on a roof-ridge and came within a bald man's eyelash of tumbling through an open skylight. And then – most embarrassing of all for a tick-tock lad of my experience – I messed up a perfectly simple Peabody Roll manoeuvre, overshooting the end gable and ending up sprawling on a flat roof beyond.

Luckily I'd instinctively protected the haversack containing the headmaster's package with one arm as I fell. But although there was no damage done, as I climbed to my feet and dusted myself down, I was angry that I had been so inept. Archimedes Barnett had entrusted the safe delivery of this specimen to me and I didn't intend to betray that trust.

Resolving to take far more care as I continued on my journey, I set off at a gentler pace and arrived at Grassington Hall School a little under an hour later with no further mishaps. It was late afternoon by the time I reached the gatehouse. The sun was low in the sky, casting long shadows across the grounds of the school and turning the pale-grey stone walls the colour of spiced honey. The 'fish-stew' fog, so dense and acrid down at the docks, was now no more than a distant memory – and with it, I believed, the horrors that had so unnerved me on the wharfside.

I called a cheery greeting to the gatekeeper. He doffed his cap and waved me through, into the school grounds. A game of Farrow Fives was once again in full swing on the main field, to the accompaniment of loud shouting and whooping from what looked like almost the entire school. As I strode past the swaying willows and spreading oaks, the sounds of cheering voices filling the air – chanting, laughing, singing – I was struck once more by just how fortunate the pupils of Grassington Hall seemed to be.

'Enter!' Archimedes Barnett called out in response to my knock on his study door.

I turned the handle and went in, to see the headmaster sitting at his desk with a large leather-bound book open in front of him and a magnifying glass clasped in one hand. He looked up.

'Barnaby!' he exclaimed. 'You've made excellent time. I congratulate you, my boy.' He tapped a finger on a magnificent engraving in the book. 'Audley-Bishop's *Birds of the Rainforests*, plate number seventy-three: the catincatapetl,' he murmured reverently, 'or *emerald messenger of darkness* – named after the Toltec demon god Catincatapetl, Master of the Underworld and Lord of Chaos.' He fixed me with a stare. 'Do you know how rare this bird is?'

I shook my head as I opened my haversack and carefully took out the small crate.

'No, of course you don't. How could you?' chuckled the headmaster, greedily seizing the box and examining its wooden sides minutely. 'If you'll excuse me, Barnaby, I must go to the bird hall at once and unpack our illustrious guest with the greatest care imaginable . . . Here.'

He fumbled in his waistcoat and drew out three large banknotes, thrusting them into my hand.

'But, Headmaster,' I protested, 'that's far too much . . .'

'Nonsense, nonsense,' Archimedes Barnett called over his shoulder to me, brushing my objections to one side as he strode out of his study and along the corridor. 'You've made an old ornithologist very happy.'

I shook my head as I made my way outside, the banknotes neatly folded in the top left-hand pocket of my poacher's waistcoat. I'd wanted to tell the headmaster about the strange ship and the bloody stain on my hand, but he hadn't given me a chance. He was just delighted to get his hands on his precious bird, no questions asked.

And if *he* was satisfied, then so was I. I'd

been rewarded handsomely for my trouble, the *Ipanema* had left the docks and the head-master had his parcel.

Job done. Or so I thought . . .

I couldn't have been more wrong if I'd baited an elephant trap with a mouse. Not that I knew it that beautiful sunny evening as I strode across the playing fields of Grassington Hall towards the gates.

I was just passing the main field when a groan went up from the crowd. I glanced across to see a boy in grass-stained flannels rolling around by one of the targets, clutching his head. There was a heavy leather ball lying by his right foot. A loud whistle sounded and a tall, heavily built man with bushy hair, ruddy cheeks and watery blue eyes came striding over.

'A fine save, Thompson,' he shouted sarcastically. 'But next time you might try stopping the ball with your hands, not your head!'

There were sniggers from the watching

pupils as the tall games master stood over the youth. It was the fair-haired boy who'd been my guide on my first visit to the school.

'Come on, Thompson!' The master prodded the prone boy with a muddy boot. 'Stop rolling around like a Highfield lady with a touch of the vapours . . .'

I pushed through the crowd and knelt by my stricken friend. Gently I pulled his hand from his face and examined the nasty-looking swelling above his left eye.

'Better get yourself off to the infirmary and have Matron look at it,' I advised Thompson, who was blinking up at me, a dazed expression on his face.

'On your feet!' bellowed the master. '*Now!*'

'Y-y-yes, sir, Mr Cripps,' Thompson mumbled, trying to get up.

I helped him climb unsteadily to his feet. 'This boy is in no condition to continue,' I protested.

Mr Cripps turned on me, his face red with suppressed rage. '*I'm* the games master!' he shouted. 'And I decide who's fit or not fit to continue. Thompson is up next, as fifth hitter – or Ibis House loses the game!'

'Not if I take his place,' I said smoothly, slipping off my topcoat and rolling up my sleeves.

A cheer went up from the crowd as the games master blustered about substitutions and second-half rules and how he had never seen me on the fives field before.

'The name's Grimes,' I told him, winking at Thompson, who was being helped to the sideline, 'and I'm a new boy, you could say.'

Again the crowd roared their approval. Mr Cripps blew his whistle and shouted, 'Well, get on with it, then, Grimes!'

I strode over to the plate, picked up the fives bat and glanced around the field. From what I'd picked up during my brief observation of the game, my task was to hit one of the targets in the outfield, where a catcher with a long-netted stick stood waiting. The shot would determine how much of a free run I'd have to get round the bases, before the opposing team were allowed to tackle me or trip me up with the fives mallets – or 'toe-crushers' – they brandished. If the ball was caught, then I was out, and it was game over.

I glanced across at Mr Cripps. From the glint in those watery blue eyes of his, I had the feeling he intended to teach me a lesson. As referee, he wouldn't find it hard.

A hush descended as the pitcher stepped forward on the playing field. The farthest target from me would give me three bases before the tacklers could move. It was my best shot.

I nodded, and the pitcher lobbed a nasty-looking screwball my way. I stepped back, giving it air, then swung the bat in a graceful arc with all my might.

I stepped back . . . then swung the bat in a graceful arc with all my might.

THWACK!

The bat and ball connected sweetly, and the crowd *oohed!* then *aahed!* as the ball flew over the target keeper and thudded into the three-base target. Flinging away the bat, I was off round the bases at a nervous trot as the tacklers, rooted to their field positions, waited like chained lurchers eyeing a mad March hare.

Peeeeep!

Cripps's whistle sounded as my foot hit third base. A trifle early, I thought – but I wasn't about to complain. Not with five tacklers tearing towards me from the four corners of the field, waving their mallets at knee height.

Whoosh!

I jumped over the first mallet and swerved past a second. The third and fourth tacklers collided with the fifth in their eagerness to get at me. The home base was in front of me as, on the sidelines, the members of Ibis

House cheered wildly and threw their tasselled caps in the air. I was going to score a home dodge, and an eagle's eye at that!

All at once, out of nowhere – like a brick wall or a fog-smothered chimney stack – Mr Cripps rose up in front of me, his red, snarling face bearing down and his great ham-like hands outstretched. It was obstruction, plain and simple, but since he was the referee, there was no point appealing. Instead, at the last moment, I dropped into a perfectly executed Peabody Roll, straight through the great oaf's legs, and up again.

Crash!

The schoolmaster bit the dust behind me with a shout of rage as I trotted on to home base and the congratulations of my team-mates!

I left them to enjoy the victory and took off before old Cripps started asking awkward questions, and was back in the bustling heart of the city as the newspaper hawkers were hitting the streets with the late editions.

'Read all about it!' they were shouting above the babble of voices and clatter of carriage wheels. 'Ghost ship found on mudbank!'

Tired as I was, and ready for my bed, that got my attention all right. I stopped one of the newspaper hawkers and bought a copy. As I stood beneath the gaslight on the corner of Ox Bucket Lane, it was all I could do to keep my hands from shaking when I read the inky black newsprint.

The *Ipanema*, a merchant sailing vessel, was found grounded on the mudbanks just south of the Spruton Bill lighthouse this morning by a party of fishermen. The ship was deserted, apparently abandoned by its entire crew. Their hasty and chaotic departure was indicated by upturned tables, meals left half eaten and, most singular of all, a blood-stained boat-hook pinning a banknote to the door of the captain's cabin . . .

CHAPTER 5

*N*eedless to say, I didn't get much sleep that night in my attic rooms, and what little I did get was disturbed by dreams of ghostly ships, wild-eyed captains and bloody cargo hooks. When at last I tumbled out of my bed and dashed some water in my face, I knew I had some decisions to make.

Should I go to the authorities and inform them of my visit to the *Ipanema*? Or should I return to Archimedes Barnett and tell him of my experiences? The more I thought about it, the less point there seemed to be to either course of action. After all, what *had* I seen? A half-crazed captain and a blood-stained cargo hook. Where the captain and his crew were now was anybody's guess.

If I – a humble tick-tock lad – went to the harbour authorities with a story like that, who knows how they might twist it round? I might even be seen as a suspect. And for what? A small crate containing an emerald bird.

As for the headmaster, if he read the report in the paper, he could go to the powers that be if he wished, but somehow I didn't think he would. He had his precious specimen and seemed happy enough. I've seen my fair share of strange and terrible things in this great heaving city – from sewers infested with flesh-eating salamanders to rooftops haunted by blood-crazed night wolves. By comparison, a crew deserting its ship seemed pretty unremarkable.

Yet there was something about that abandoned ship and the disembodied voice in the fog that kept playing on my mind. In the end

I resolved to research ghost ships and mysterious portents on my next visit to Underhill's
Library for Scholars of the Arcane. First,
though, I had to pay a visit to my good
friend Professor Pinkerton-Barnes, who
had summoned me on a matter of some
urgency.

I highstacked it across town to the tall
university building where he worked. There
was a fine drizzle falling by the time I
reached the lofty slate turret. I slid down
the thin, ridged drainpipe, landed lightly on
a third-floor window ledge and climbed into
the professor's laboratory.

Professor Pinkerton-Barnes – or PB to his
friends – was at the far end of the laboratory, bent over his cluttered desk, one eye
clamped to a microscope.

'Morning, PB,' I called.

The professor looked up, his shock of
white hair quivering. 'Oh, Barnaby, it's you,'
he said. 'Is it really too much to ask you to

use the door once in a while?'

He climbed to his feet, groaning slightly and muttering about his 'aching old bones' as he did so, and walked round the desk.

'PB,' I said as he approached. 'Your eyebrow!'

The professor's hand shot upwards, and he rubbed the hairless ridge above his left eye.

'Yes, yes,' he muttered. 'A rather unfortunate accident with a Bunsen burner. But I dare say it'll grow back . . .'

I hoped it would. The professor's expression, fixed in a state of semi-surprise, was rather unnerving.

'But this is all by the by,' he went on, 'and not at all the reason why I summoned you, Barnaby. I have a job of some urgency for you.'

I nodded. 'Always happy to oblige,' I said.

'I have this theory . . .' the professor began, and I had to smile.

If I had a mallard's egg for every time I'd

heard those words, I could make an omelette the size of a duck pond. The professor was full of far-fetched theories – everything from the idea that water voles were learning to walk upright because of overgrown canal paths, to bullfinches attacking cats after eating the fruit of the oriental tilberry tree. Most of them proved without foundation, and I should know, because the professor employed me to test them.

But I shouldn't be too sceptical. Every so often the professor was spot on. Like the time he proved that the distilled gizzards of an arctic ptarmigan could cure a bad case of cerebral hives – one theory I was personally delighted to prove . . .

'You do?' I said, suppressing my smile.

'Indeed, Barnaby,' said the professor, squinting at me with his newly acquired quizzical expression. 'My theory is that a week's worth of soiled lab coats will have been freshly laundered and expertly ironed, and will now be awaiting collection at the Lotus Blossom Laundry in Chinatown ...'

He fished in the pocket of the admittedly grubby, not to say singed, lab coat he presently wore, and produced a crumpled laundry receipt.

'Would you care to prove my theory correct?' the professor said with a laugh.

'It would be my pleasure, PB,' I replied, plucking the receipt from his fingers and slipping out of the window. As I climbed up the drainpipe, I heard the professor call after me.

'And remind me to acquaint you with my theory of doors and stairs some time ...'

I highstacked it across town in no time, skirting the Wasps' Nest quarter and crossing the theatre district. The rain had cleared, and I arrived in Chinatown in sunshine. Performing an ambitious leap from the end gable of a tall almshouse, I found myself on the roof of the Lotus Blossom

Laundry, slightly winded, but otherwise in one piece.

I sat for a few moments on the broad sloping roof with its glazed green slates, and caught my breath. Then, feeling rather hungry, I pulled a small bag from the left-hand pocket of my topcoat and a bottle of ginger ale from the right-hand one. The bag contained a hot wrapped parcel. I unwrapped the greaseproof paper gingerly. As I did so, the pasty it contained released its wonderful aromas – aromas so scrumptious my mouth watered. The pasty was a Stover's Special – especially designed for the men who worked at the great coal furnaces.

I'd had the foresight to pick one up on my way over to the professor's. After all, I reasoned as I took a bite, I had to keep my strength up, didn't I?

I took another bite from the half of the pasty that was decorated with a pastry leaf. That was the half that contained a savoury mixture of lamb, carrots and turnips. I took several more mouthfuls, wiping the salty gravy from my chin with my handkerchief. Then, when I reached the little dividing wall of pastry in the middle, I paused, unstoppered the ginger ale and took a swig. The second half of the pasty was filled with a sweet, spiced apple mixture, dripping with syrup and laden with plump sultanas.

'Delicious,' I muttered to myself. I brushed the crumbs from the front of my waistcoat, finished off the ginger ale and climbed to my feet.

It's strange that such a simple meal, eaten up on the rooftops under the warm mid-morning sun, should have proved so memorable. Yet it has. Perhaps because I associate it with one of the most remarkable episodes in my life, and a meeting with someone who would change me for ever. To this day, I only have to catch the smell of a Stover's Special to be transported back to the Lotus Blossom Laundry in Chinatown on that fateful day . . .

I climbed down from the rooftop into a side alley, hot and humid from the laundry steam vents, and turned the corner to enter the laundry by the front door. Great West Street, the main thoroughfare of Chinatown, was as crowded as usual. Shops of every type and description thronged with people, as did the myriad market stalls that lined the broad road.

Moneychangers, letter writers, bird sellers and silk merchants touted for trade alongside herbalists, fortune-tellers and firework makers. However many times I passed through Chinatown, I never tired of its sights and sounds – the brightly painted statues of its gaudy temples, the delicious odours wafting up from cellar dining halls and the glowing lanterns that decked every lintel and doorway.

Pausing to retrieve the professor's laundry receipt from my top waistcoat pocket, I pushed open the heavy rosewood door of the laundry and entered.

A large paper lantern cast a yellow glow over the high-ceilinged chamber, which was lined on three sides by huge shelves piled high with neatly folded laundry. Facing me across the tiled floor was a broad counter, at which sat an elderly Chinese man with a long, stringy white beard and a tall hat of folded paper perched on his head.

Behind him, a great glass window revealed the cavernous laundry beyond, teeming with an army of laundresses clustered round copper vats of boiling water, troughs frothing with soapsuds, and giant mangles that took five pairs of arms to turn. Beneath his tall paper hat, Chung Lee – the laundry's owner – didn't notice me come in. He seemed to have his hands full with a heavy, thick-set customer in a velvet jacket and green Epsom, who was jabbing a stubby finger into the laundry owner's chest to emphasize what he was saying.

'My point is, Mr Lee,' the jug-eared thug said with a jab that made Chung Lee's paper hat wobble, 'you don't have till next month to pay up. Or next week. Or, for that matter' – he jabbed again – 'till tomorrow. You pay up *now*, understand?'

'But your friend, the little one, he say, "Pay next month,"' the laundry owner protested weakly. 'I don't have money now . . .'

Jug-Ears pushed the brim of his green Epsom back on his close-shaven head with a stubby finger, then made a fist.

'I'm beginning to lose my temper, Mr Lee,' he snarled.

I'd seen this sort of shakedown a thousand times before, and it made my blood boil. Jumped-up strongman using his muscle to squeeze protection money out of tradesmen. The thug was even dressed for the part in his vulgar velvet jacket and felt-covered hard hat. Probably had a cosh and a knuckle-

duster in the pockets of his embroidered
waistcoat. I wasn't taking any chances. I
flicked the catch on the handle of my cane
and unsheathed my sword, before tapping
the thug lightly on the shoulder.

'What the—?' he grunted in surprise as he
turned to find a steel blade pointed at his
chest.

'I'd be on my way if I were you,' I said
coolly, although inside I could feel my anger
rising like steam in a linen press.

Jug-Ear's eyes narrowed and his lip curled.
'A tick-tock lad!' he sneered. 'Are you old
enough to be playing with sharp swords,
sonny?'

In answer I gave a deft flick of my wrist,
and my sword tip plucked the green Epsom
from his shaven head, sending it clattering to
the tiled floor. With a downward cut, I sliced
the ivory buttons off his waistcoat – and sure
enough, a leather cosh and iron knuckle-
duster fell out and clattered to the floor, to

join the green hat.

'Why, you—' Jug-Ears began, but backed away when he saw, by the look in my eyes, that I meant business.

'All right, sonny, no need to fight. I'm sure Mr Lee's got enough to pay us both off . . .'

He stopped, his eyes narrowed again, and then a big stupid grin spread over the thug's oafish face. If it hadn't been for that gap-toothed grin, I'd have been a goner. As it was, I managed to half turn when the attack from behind came. It caught me a glancing blow instead of staving my skull in.

I was sent clattering to the floor, where I lay dazed alongside the tools of the thug's trade. Looking up, I saw that Jug-Ears had been joined by a small, ratty-looking companion in equally gaudy clothes. He must have slipped in behind me and felled me with a coward's blow from the ugly-looking cudgel he grasped in both hands.

'Can't leave you alone for two minutes,

Fegg, without you getting turned over by a
. . . a tick-tock lad!'

'Sorry, but he snuck up behind me,'
Jug-Ears protested, retrieving his hat.

'Well, now I've snuck up behind him, ain't
I?' said Ratface with an unpleasant smirk as
he raised the cudgel above his head. 'And he's
going to get what's coming to him—'

'And what would that be, gentlemen?'
came a soft, lilting voice from behind the
counter.

I looked up to see a small, waif-like girl
standing beside Mr Lee, her hands clasped at
her front and head cocked demurely to one
side. Despite the predicament I was in, I
couldn't help noticing how beautiful she was.
She had black plaits, milky skin, bright
flashing eyes and the daintiest nose I've ever
seen.

'Run along, missy,' Jug-Ears told her. 'This
is nothing to do with you.'

'Oh, but I think it is,' she replied sweetly.

'Mei Ling, please,' said Chung Lee.

But the girl simply smiled. 'My grand-father and I are as close as' – she held up her hand and crossed her first two fingers – 'this! You have a problem with my grandfather, you have a problem with me! So I suggest that it is you two who "run along".'

Suddenly Jug-Ears lost his temper completely. 'I warned you!' he snarled, picking up the leather cosh and swinging it at her head.

Mei Ling ducked, the smile never faltering for a moment. Jug-Ears swung the cosh again. This time Mei Ling jumped up onto the counter and stepped daintily to one side as the oaf brought the cosh smashing down onto the polished wooden surface. He howled with pain as the impact of the blow jarred his shoulder. Mei Ling looked down at him, smiling that broad, beautiful smile of hers.

'I really think you should just leave,' she said.

Mei Ling looked down at him, smiling that broad, beautiful smile of hers.

For a moment he stood there, a mixture of rage and confusion plucking his face in all directions. The girl winked. Outraged, the thug tried to grab her ankles. Instead, she leaped up, performed an effortless double-somersault in midair, and landed behind him.

Jug-Ears spun round, slashing and swiping at her with the cosh, joined this time by his rat-faced companion. Mei Ling avoided the blows of the cudgel and the cosh with another effortless leap, high in the air, over the glowing paper lantern, before landing silently at my side. I reached for my swordstick, but Mei Ling stopped me with a slight shake of her head and a delicate frown.

Instead, she turned and confronted Ratface and Jug-Ears, who were lumbering towards her, both red in the face and panting from their useless exertions. Mei Ling stopped them in their tracks with an unblinking stare and a raised finger. Then, from between her beautiful lips, came a soft, lilting hum – like the drone of a dragonfly. She moved her finger from side to side and, like salivating guard dogs eyeing a bone, the eyes of the two thugs followed it.

'Now, you're not going to hurt my grand-father, *are* you?' she said softly.

'No,' they grunted in unison, 'we're not going to hurt your grandfather.'

'You're going to leave, and never come back, aren't you?'

'Leave and never come back,' they intoned, their heads nodding as she raised and lowered her finger.

'Excellent,' said Mei Ling, lowering her arm and clapping her hands together like someone wiping dust from their palms.

The two of them climbed slowly to their feet. Then, as meek and mild as a pair of whipped dogs, their tails between their legs, they laid their weapons down on the floor and shuffled across the room to the door. Ratface went out first, with Jug-Ears closing the door quietly behind him as he brought up the rear.

As the catch clicked shut, it was as though a spell was broken. I turned to Mei Ling.

'That was absolutely incredible,' I said. 'Amazing . . . How on earth did you do that?'

She smiled that beautiful smile of hers. 'Grandfather doesn't approve. He calls it "showing off",' she said with a giggle. 'He prefers it if I hand them an empty purse and tell them it is full.'

From the counter Chung Lee nodded, his paper hat wobbling, and held out a hand for the professor's laundry receipt. Getting to my feet, I sheathed my sword and handed him the piece of paper – only for Mei Ling to snatch it from my fingers with another delightful giggle.

'The laundry can wait,' she told me. 'Are you the tick-tock lad I saw eating his lunch on the roof?'

I smiled. 'The very same,' I said. 'Barnaby

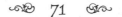

Grimes. Pleased to meet you.'

I held out a hand, but Mei Ling ignored it.

'And you want to know how I dealt with our unwelcome visitors just now?'

I nodded.

'You must promise me something in return,' she said.

'Yes?' I said, intrigued.

'You must promise,' she said with a tinkling laugh, 'to tell me what you were eating . . . It looked absolutely delicious!'

CHAPTER

6

For the next few days I set about my tick-tock rounds with renewed purpose. Turning out the contents of my bureau, I went to work in a fresh shirt and waistcoat each day. As I highstacked all over town, delivering parcels and documents, I brushed past sooty chimneys at every opportunity, rolled across countless dusty rooftops and dined carelessly on wharfman's stew. Soon I had a suitably impressive bundle of laundry – and I knew just where to deliver it.

Rising early three days later, I climbed out of my attic window and shinned up onto the roof, eager to renew my acquaintance with the beautiful young laundress.

A watery, pale sun shone down through an early morning haze, and as I glanced up, I suddenly remembered the remarkable occurrence PB had been talking about excitedly all year. At the end of the summer there was to be an eclipse of the sun.

'A full eclipse, Barnaby,' he'd informed me, his eyes twinkling. 'The first for ninety-eight years! Think about it, my boy. The sun completely extinguished. Day turned to night!'

Gazing up at the sun that morning, I realized that Mei Ling had banished any thought of the eclipse from my head. And just about every other thought, for that matter. As I crossed the rooftops, I could hear the familiar cries of the street vendors and market spielers plying their trade on the roads below.

'What do you lack? What do you lack?'

the words echoed up through the smoky air.

'Fresh milk by the ladle! Penny a dip!'

'Orchard apples, ripe and cheap!'

I was above the corner of Pettigrew Street and Leinster Lane when I heard the cry I'd been listening out for. Leaping from the gutter I was perched upon, down to the jutting window ledge below me, I performed a move the great Tom Flint had taught me a few years earlier – the Flying Fox, it was called; a tricky manoeuvre which involved a flagpole, an unbuttoned coat and a steady nerve. Seconds later, I landed on the pavement beside a portly pieman, a tray of steaming pies and pasties around his neck.

'Two Stover's Specials,' I said, and dropped a couple of coppers into his outstretched hand.

Back up on the rooftops, I paused briefly at the old Guildhall and surveyed the horizon before setting off once more. The bell at the top of the Corn Exchange was chiming seven o'clock as I crossed Bowery Road, which marked the northernmost boundary to Chinatown. Fifty yards ahead was the green roof of the Lotus Blossom Laundry, its glazed tiles glistening with raindrops from the previous night's downpour.

The architecture of the building had been borrowed from the orient. Tall whitewashed walls were topped with a mansard roof, upswept eaves and undulating gables. Adjusting the bulging sack of laundry strapped to my back, I made my way across the rooftop, and was about to select a drain-pipe for my descent when a mullioned window beneath the eaves opened and Mei Ling's head poked out.

'Barnaby Grimes,' she called over to me, her face breaking into a smile. 'I've been expecting you. The water is just coming to the boil.'

Expecting me? I wondered. Water coming to the boil? How on earth could she have known I would visit at that moment?

My confusion must have shown on my face, for the next moment Mei Ling broke into a peal of laughter. 'Come in, come in,' she said. 'And bring that bundle of laundry with you.'

I jumped across the gap between the two buildings and swung down over the eaves onto the sill of Mei Ling's window. She stepped aside and motioned for me to enter. I took off my coalstack hat, clicked it flat and entered a richly furnished salon.

The floor was of dark mahogany with intricate inlays of pale silver birch, and strewn with finely woven mats of seagrass. The walls were painted in white, red and gold, with emerald-green dragons writhing across their surface, and the huge attic room was divided into smaller sections with the aid of tall, double-hinged screens. Waist-high

I jumped across the gap between the two buildings . . .

vases, each one elegantly painted, stood on either side of the window and at the top of the stairs on black varnished pedestals, their glazed gold and turquoise surfaces glowing in the light cast by the pink and orange paper lanterns overhead.

Mei Ling reached towards me, her arms outstretched. I stepped forward somewhat awkwardly and was about to shake her hand when she giggled and slipped past me. With a touch lighter than a racecourse pickpocket, she plucked the laundry sack from my shoulders and my swordstick from my hand, spinning me round by the sleeve to face her once more.

'This will be taken care of downstairs,' she said, placing the sack to one side. 'While this' – Mei Ling held up my swordstick and flicked back the catch to reveal the blade – 'this interests me.'

'Careful, that blade's sharp,' I warned her.

'Do you have much cause to use this?' Mei

Ling asked, unsheathing the sword and holding it up to the light.

'There have been occasions when I've had to defend myself . . .' I said guardedly.

'And this sword concealed within an innocent-looking walking stick has proved useful?' Mei Ling said. 'Show me.'

She handed the sword to me and stepped back, her arms folded.

'Show you? But how?' I shrugged.

'By touching me on the shoulder with the tip of your blade.' Mei Ling smiled, her dark eyes glinting mischievously.

'Just touch you on the shoulder?' I said, making sure I'd understood.

Mei Ling nodded.

I raised my sword and was about to tap her right shoulder lightly when she stepped to one side. Spinning round, I tried again, only for Mei Ling to swerve elegantly past me, whispering in my ear as she did so.

'Come on, Barnaby. Try harder . . .'

I turned and feinted to my left, flicking my sword arm out at the last moment. Mei Ling leaped high to avoid the sword cut, only to land on the tip of the blade for an instant – her elegant slippered foot balanced on tiptoe – before somersaulting over my head. She tapped me on the shoulder, her beautiful face wreathed in smiles.

'I'm sorry, Barnaby,' she laughed. 'I'm showing off. My grandfather says it is my worst trait.'

I turned to her and sheathed my sword. 'How do you do that?' I asked, astonished at her acrobatics. 'My old friend Tom Flint could balance on a rusty gutter two inches wide, but not on the tip of a sword . . .'

Mei Ling motioned for me to sit at a low table by the window that had been laid for tea.

Sitting down opposite me, she leaned forward and, with a charming frown of concentration, opened the cork stopper of a tall pot and put one wooden spoonful of the pale green powder it contained into each of the two handleless cups before us. As she did so, a sweet, mossy aroma filled my nostrils. Then, with the same calm attention to detail, she grasped the raffia handle of the bulbous copper teapot, which was steaming gently over a tea light, and poured boiling water into the cups, one after the other. The aroma grew more intense as a thin twist of steam rose up from the surface of the liquid. It was like no tea I had ever smelled before.

'What is it?' I asked.

'Green tea,' she told me, without looking up. 'Fortified with ginseng and scented with jasmine.'

Having returned the teapot to the cradle above the flickering flame of the tea light, she picked up a small whisk, fashioned from wood and dried twine, and gently beat the liquid before laying the whisk to one side.

I reached out to take the steaming cup of tea in front of me – only to be stilled by Mei Ling.

'Wait,' she said. 'First, look into the steam that rises from the tea. See how it twists and writhes . . . Really concentrate, Barnaby . . . Concentrate . . .' Mei Ling's voice whispered hypnotically in my ear.

I did what she said. As I stared at the ever-shifting column of dancing mist, something strange started to take place. It was as though the wisps of steam were taking on a certain solidity – like silken scarves, like dragonfly wings, like a fountain rising up into the air and disappearing.

'Now, look into the spaces in the mist . . .'

Sure enough, I found my gaze focusing on the spaces – like long tunnels opening up and spiralling away into the distance – between those twisting, writhing wisps of steam . . .

'Barnaby . . .' I heard my name filtering into my consciousness. 'Barnaby . . .' Mei

Ling's voice was soft and melodic, and it was followed by the sound of hands lightly clapping. 'Barnaby Grimes.'

I looked up to see Mei Ling staring back at me, her eyes sparkling with amusement. She clapped her hands a second time, in that curious way of hers, as if wiping dust from her fingers.

'M . . . Mei Ling,' I said softly. I felt almost as though I was wakening from sleep.

'That is your first lesson in yinchido.' She smiled, handing me the teacup.

'Yinchido?' I said, taking a sip of the tea. It tasted as good as it smelled.

'Yinchido,' she repeated. 'The Way of the Silver Mist. It is an ancient art that has been practised for centuries in the remote mountains of my homeland. The art of absence . . .'

'I . . . I don't understand,' I said.

Mei Ling took a sip of her tea. 'You have already glimpsed the principle of yinchido when you looked into the gaps in the steam.'

I looked down at my gently steaming teacup.

'You see, Barnaby,' she went on, 'we use our senses to detect sights, sounds, smells . . . But the world is more than that. It is also about what *isn't* there.'

I frowned.

'There is what we *can* see, but also what we *cannot* see. There are sounds, but there is also silence. There is touch,' she said, reaching out and running the tip of a finger down my cheek. She smiled and pulled away. 'But there is also the feeling of not being touched. To understand either properly, we must know both. Most people only experience what their senses tell them is there. Yinchido teaches us to appreciate what isn't there – the spaces.'

My head spun as I tried to grasp exactly what she was saying.

'So,' I said, 'in a fight, you would step into the spaces to avoid an attacker? Just as you did to avoid my sword – and when those two great oafs attacked you the other day . . .'

Mei Ling nodded.

'But then you didn't just *avoid* their attacks,' I pursued. 'You seemed to control their minds . . .'

Mei Ling looked intently into my eyes. 'As I told you, Barnaby, yinchido is about using spaces,' she said in a quiet voice. 'Physical spaces are one thing, but there are also mental spaces. I stepped into the mental spaces of those two bad men and filled them with my own wishes . . .'

'You make it sound so simple,' I said in awe.

'The Way of the Silver Mist is a long path, Barnaby,' she told me softly. 'But if you wish to take it, I would be happy to be your guide.'

I nodded enthusiastically and took another

sip of the tea, only for my stomach to rumble with hunger.

'I almost forgot, I brought you these,' I laughed, reaching into my pockets and pulling out the Stover's pasties. 'I find they're excellent at filling empty spaces!'

An hour later, I climbed out of the attic window of the laundry with a bundle of crisp, pressed shirts and waistcoats, a jar of green tea and a set of instructions from my beautiful guide.

Each morning I brewed my own tea and concentrated on the steam rising as it cooled. Each evening I sat on the rooftop of my attic rooms and practised the breathing exercises Mei Ling had given me, searching for pockets of silence lurking in amidst the noise of the city as I did so.

Strange as it may seem, as that long hot summer passed, these simple techniques began to make a difference. My highstacking benefited for a start. I no longer seemed to take the tumbles and falls that every high-stacker must expect in the course of his rounds and, with the absence of cuts and bruises, I became more confident of even the trickier manoeuvres. My swordplay improved too, although I also found I could anticipate and avoid trouble far more easily as my powers of concentration grew. And finally, I was never without a stack of freshly laundered shirts.

Mei Ling was so pleased with my progress that she began to teach me about the power of the mind and yinchido techniques to enhance it. It was fascinating stuff and I was looking forward to an enlightening autumn with my beautiful guide.

Unfortunately, that was not to be. Dark forces were at work, an ancient evil was spreading, and I – for all my yinchido training – didn't see it coming.

Turning the corner into Grevy Lane one

morning late that summer, I walked into a shambling character hurrying in the opposite direction. He looked into my eyes, an expression of abject terror on his face, like a rat in a tuppenny trap.

'It's you!' I gasped.

CHAPTER 7

It was none other than the Major, the amiable gatekeeper from Grassington Hall – though until I'd looked into his eyes, I hadn't recognized him, so dramatically had he changed.

He was unwashed, dishevelled and as pungent as a tomcat, and there were deep scratches on his head and hands. His once neat side-whiskers were matted and filthy, his waxed moustache now bristled like a scullery maid's broom, while his face was so haggard it looked as if he hadn't slept for a year. There were buttons missing from his jacket, and a tear in one of the knees of his breeches, the frayed tatters of cloth fringed with dried blood where he'd fallen and cut his leg.

'Little horrors, little horrors, little horrors . . .' he was muttering to himself as he brushed against my shoulder, and he would have passed me by if I hadn't grabbed the sleeve of his jacket with an outstretched arm.

'You're the Major, from Grassington Hall, aren't you?' I asked him.

At the sound of my words, the poor man froze. He turned his head slowly towards me, until his terrified gaze was fixed on my own eyes. His gaunt face went as white as a pastry-cook's apron and the right side of his mouth began to twitch involuntarily.

'The gatekeeper,' I persisted. 'At Grass-ington Hall?'

The man looked stricken. He started back, fine beads of sweat on his forehead. 'Y-you're not . . .' he stammered. 'You're not one of them, are you?' His voice was low, tremulous, and so full of dread you'd have thought he'd just seen a ghost.

'Them?' I said.

'I'm not going back there.' He trembled, his eyes taking on a hunted, panic-stricken look. 'Never, you hear me? Never . . .' His voice was becoming hysterical. 'And they can't make me . . .'

With those words, he tore my hand from his sleeve and pushed past me. Out of the alley he clattered, his hobnail boots skidding on the cobbles as he ran, before darting out across the road – straight into the path of an oncoming coach-and-four which, at that exact moment, came thundering round the corner.

'Watch out!' I bellowed.

But too late. A moment later, there was a thud, a crunch and an agonized scream, followed by panicked whinnying, and the sound of the coachman cracking his whip and bellowing for his rearing horses to calm down.

'Easy there! *Easy!*'

The stamping of hooves and rattle of the iron wheels came to an abrupt standstill. I looked across the pavement, my heart in my mouth, to see the gatekeeper lying motionless in the gutter, one arm twisted behind his head, his legs broken and crumpled beneath him, and a line of blood trickling from the corner of his mouth. Passers-by rushed over to see what could be done, but as I joined them, I already knew it was hopeless.

I looked down into the gatekeeper's terror-filled eyes; his lips twitched as he struggled to speak.

'Evil . . . Terrible evil . . .' he rasped. 'Beware . . .'

His head jerked forward urgently, before falling to one side, and his eyes glazed over into a sightless stare as he breathed his last.

A sizeable crowd had now gathered around

the stricken gatekeeper, gawping and chattering. The coachman had climbed down from his seat and was telling anyone who would listen the same thing, over and over.

'He just ran out in front of me. Just ran out, he did. There was nothing I could do. He just ran out in front of me . . .'

Others took up the same refrain – an old woman with a basket; a dairymaid with a couple of buckets of milk yoked across her shoulders – everyone seemed in agreement.

'Didn't look where he was going . . .'

'He just ran out in front of him . . .'

'Looked like a madman, poor soul . . .'

A police constable, red-faced and wheezing, barged his way through the milling crowd.

'Mind your backs,' he shouted as he elbowed onlookers aside. 'Move along now, please. Nothing more to see.' Standing over the dead body, he pulled a notebook and a pencil from his back pocket. 'Now, can anyone tell me exactly what happened?'

'He didn't look. Just ran out into the street . . .' the dairymaid began.

'There was nothing I could do,' came the gruff voice of the coachman, repeating himself. 'Just ran out, he did . . .'

Slipping back into the crowd, I left them to it. One more crazy beggar coming to grief on the cobbles of Market Street, busiest thoroughfare in the great bustling city. 'Carriage carrion', such casualties were called, and this poor wretch was just one more of them. The difference was that a few weeks ago, this madman had been sane and rational and cheerfully tending the gate at a respectable private school.

What had gone wrong?

The incident had brought me down to earth with a bump. While I'd spent all summer with my head full of laundry tickets and Stover's pasties, mental gymnastics and sweet smiles, something had gone badly wrong at Grassington Hall. Of course, I had to find out what. But first I needed something to settle my nerves.

Crossing the snarled-up traffic of Market Street, I headed down Cannery Row and stepped into the reassuring wood-panelled gloom of Marconi's Coffee House. Ordering a cup of Black Java, I breathed in the rich coffee aroma and tried to make sense of what I'd just witnessed.

'Barnaby?' A hearty voice broke into my thoughts. 'Barnaby Grimes. My dear fellow, good to see you!'

Looking up, I saw that the voice belonged to a regular client of mine – a portly, ruddy-cheeked coal merchant by the name of Sidney Cruikshank – seated at the next table. Together with his brother, he owned Cruikshank and Cruikshank, the coal merchant's next door to Marconi's.

Throughout the autumn and early winter, their huge carthorses would deliver vast loads of coal all over the city, recouping the money week by week throughout the rest of the year. My job in the last week of summer was to take the advance orders for the season ahead. We tick-tock lads called it 'coal scuttling', and it was one of our busiest times of the year.

'Morning, Mr Cruikshank,' I said, a little weakly.

'Good morning to you, Barnaby,' he said, his loud voice drowning out the babble of conversation in the coffee house. He reached across and thrust out a great ham of a hand, the nails and creases black with coal dust. 'You must drop by – the new season's almost upon us, my boy.'

'Certainly,' I said, and sighed.

Mr Cruikshank frowned and thrust his huge red face close to mine. 'Are you all right, old son? If you don't mind my saying, you're looking a bit peaky. Not coming down with something, I trust?'

I shook my head. 'I've just seen a man get

run over on Market Street,' I told him.

Mr Cruikshank breathed in noisily through his teeth. 'Dreadful, dreadful,' he said, shaking his head sympathetically. 'The roads these days. Not a coal dray, I hope . . .'

'A coach-and-four,' I said. 'Ran over a beggar.'

'Carriage carrion!' said Cruikshank with a snort. 'When will these people learn? One must take care crossing a busy street . . .'

'I knew him, actually,' I said. 'Up till quite recently he was the gatekeeper at Grassington Hall School.'

'Grassington Hall, eh?' said Cruikshank, arching an eyebrow. 'Mighty fine academic institution. And I should know. I send young Sidney junior there.'

The news surprised me – although come to think of it, I realized I hadn't seen the young Cruikshank lad at his father's offices for quite some time. He was like a miniature version of his father – though, if anything, rounder and slightly redder in the face.

'In his second year,' Mr Cruikshank continued, nodding. 'Having a whale of a time, by all accounts – and getting a damn good education into the bargain.' He reached into the inside pocket of his jacket and pulled out a sheet of folded vellum. 'In fact, I received this from him not half an hour since.' He smiled. 'Tick-tock lad delivered it to me in the yard . . . Just popped into Marconi's for a cup of the black stuff and a quick read.' He looked up and flapped the letter in my face. 'Would you like to hear how he's getting on?'

I nodded – though, to be honest, I suspect he'd have told me whether I wanted to or not. He pulled a pair of steel-rimmed spectacles from his top pocket and put them on, then unfolded the letter and cleared his throat.

'*Dearest Father and Mother,*' he began. He paused and peered at me above the half-moon lenses. 'Wonderful penmanship they teach them as well.' He resumed reading, his voice a little slow as he laboured over the words. *'Dearest Father and Mother, I trust that this letter finds you in good health. I have settled in well this term. I am working very hard and learning a lot. Lessons are very interesting, the masters treat us well – and there is plenty of food. You mustn't worry about a thing. I'll make you proud of me. Your loving son, Sidney.'*

He looked up and smiled, and I detected a certain moistness in his eyes.

'You're right,' I said. 'It sounds as though he's getting on well.'

'Working hard and playing hard,' said Sidney Cruikshank. He pulled a large checked handkerchief from his jacket pocket and blew his nose noisily. 'Make me proud, he says . . . I'm telling you, Barnaby, I'm already the proudest father in the whole world. Young Sidney's getting all the advantages of a good education that I never had.'

I finished my coffee and left the coal merchant re-reading his son's letter, his eyes glistening and his lips moving as he did so. Turning left out of Marconi's, I crossed the road – taking more care than usual as I did so – and turned back down Grevy Lane. I reached the far end and was just about to shin up a conveniently sited drainpipe when I noticed a tick-tock lad looking vaguely about him, a bunch of vellum envelopes in his hand.

He wore a coalstack hat like my own, only a couple of sizes too big, and a battered and patched-up waistcoat that looked like a hand-me-down. Instead of a swordstick, he clutched a gnarled cudgel under one arm – useful for beating off troublesome guard dogs, but for little else. With his muddy boots, worn clothes and sooty face, the lad had 'cobblestone-creeper' written all over him.

'Can I help?' I said.

The lad had 'cobblestone-creeper' written all over him.

The lad turned. He saw at once, of course, that I too was a tick-tock lad, and nodded greetings.

'I'm looking for number seventy-nine,' he said, and shook his head. 'Can't seem to find it anywhere.'

'There isn't a number seventy-nine on this street,' I said. 'It stops at fifty-five.'

'But there must be,' he said. 'It's where' – he looked down at the envelope at the top of the bundle – 'a Mr and Mrs Tillstone live. Seventy-nine Garvey Lane . . .'

I laughed. The lad was either new to this game – or he was as poor with his letters as old Sidney Cruikshank. Either way, taking pity on him, I decided to put him right.

'This is *Grevy* Lane,' I said with a smile. 'Garvey Lane's the next one along. In that direction,' I added, pointing.

'Really?' he said. 'Thanks, Mr . . .'

'Barnaby.' I smiled, putting out my hand. 'Barnaby Grimes. Glad to be of service.'

The lad shook my hand enthusiastically. 'Will,' he said. 'Will Farmer.' Pushing his coalstack hat up with a grimy hand, he shrugged his shoulders. 'I'm new to this lark. In fact, this is only my second job. I was delivering some duck eggs down south – lovely countryside – when I gets called over to these gates. Big manor house or something ... And this kid gives me three gold-uns to deliver this here sack of letters ...'

Will stopped and narrowed his eyes as he looked me up and down. 'You're one of them highstackers, ain't you?' he said, his voice full of awe.

'I am,' I said, a note of pride creeping into my own voice.

He glanced up at the rooftops. 'I'd *love* to be a highstacker,' he said. 'Away from all the noise, the hustle and bustle . . . Up there among the spires and steeples ... ' He sighed, long and heartfelt, then turned to me, his face as eager and full of pleading as a Friday

cat's at a fish stall. 'I don't suppose . . . some-
time . . . not now, of course . . . you might
teach me highstacking. I mean, you must
have had a teacher yourself once . . .'

I smiled. I liked the kid's cheek.

'How did *you* get started, Barnaby?'

'I was taught by a tick-tock lad named
Tom Flint,' I told him.

I heard young Will's sharp intake of
breath. 'Not *the* Tom Flint,' he said.

'You've heard of him?' I said, impressed.
'Taught me everything I know, did Tom . . .'

'Like the Peabody Roll?' Will said, nodding
enthusiastically. 'And the Flying Fox? What
about the Rolling Derby, and the Hobson's
Choice . . . ?'

I laughed. 'You *have* been doing your
homework!'

'I certainly have,' he said. 'I don't want to
be a cobblestone-creeper for ever.' He turned
his gaze up towards the chimney stacks high
above our heads. 'I want to be up there . . .

So, will you teach me? Here's my card.'

Will scrabbled at the pockets of his worn waistcoat and fished out a handwritten card with his name and the address of a dingy mansion block in the cloth-cutters' district. He handed it to me with an eager smile.

Everybody has to start somewhere, I thought as I took the kid's card. I was a lowly bottle-black, friendless and alone, when Tom Flint crossed my path. Dropped a docket off at the bottle factory and spotted me swinging on the workshop beams while the drunken overseer slept . . .

Will's expectant eyes were on mine.

'I'm in the middle of something, kid,' I said, and saw the disappointment cloud his face like a storm at a church social. 'But I'll see what I can do . . .' I slipped the kid's card into my waistcoat pocket.

'Promise?' said Will, his face brightening.

'Promise,' I said.

He turned and darted off in the direction

of Garvey Lane as fast as his over-sized muddy boots would take him. I suppose he was afraid I might change my mind – and who knows, he was probably right. The last thing I needed just then was a fresh-faced apprentice still wet behind the ears.

I was about to shin up the drainpipe when something at my feet caught my eye. In his excitement, the young tick-tock lad had dropped one of his letters on the wet cobbles. I stooped and picked it up, only for the sodden envelope to peel open in my hands. I was just about to re-seal it – a dab of wax gum from the tin in my waistcoat would have done the trick – when the crest on the notepaper caught my attention.

Grassington Hall.

Will Farmer must have been the tick-tock lad who'd delivered Cruikshank's son's letter to his coalyard, I realized. Despite myself, with trembling fingers I pulled the letter free from the envelope, unfolded it and started reading.

Dearest Father and Mother,

I trust that this letter finds you in good health. I have settled in well this term. I am working very hard and learning a lot. Lessons are very interesting, the masters treat us well – and there is plenty of food. You mustn't worry about a thing. I'll make you proud of me.

Your loving son,
Julius

There was no doubt about it. Apart from the name at the end of the letter, it was identical to the one received by the coal merchant – even down to the penmanship.

I felt sick to my stomach. I'd seen letters like this before. It could mean only one thing. Grassington Hall had become a lock-up academy.

I shook my head. Archimedes Barnett had seemed such a decent headmaster, and his pupils had appeared so well cared for and happy. But this letter and the countless identical letters in Will's sack, with their soothing words and reassurances for parents and guardians, were ringing alarm bells in my head louder than a fire-wagon. I knew there was only one way to silence them.

I had to return to Grassington Hall to find out what had gone so terribly wrong. I left at once. After all, as we tick-tock lads say, there's no time like the present.

CHAPTER 8

It was a dark, moonless night, and as the lamplit streets gave way to the narrow hedge-lined lanes of the southern outskirts, I felt a shiver of apprehension. Ahead of me lay the great double gates of Grassington Hall, silhouetted against the starry sky. As I approached, I saw a heavy padlocked chain, like a coiled python, locking them shut.

So it was true, then, I thought ruefully. Grassington Hall was indeed a lock-up academy.

In the circumstances, there was only one thing for me to do. I had to sneak inside and get a message from one of the wretched imprisoned pupils. A scrawled note with a lock of hair or a much-loved stuffed toy would alert Dear Mama and Papa to their little angel's plight.

Lock-up academies were best nipped in the bud, in my experience. Once I'd delivered the plea for help, the parents usually did the rest, alerting the authorities to shut the place down. At the first sign of trouble, the swindlers and con artists who ran these schools usually took what they could carry and disappeared – as long, that is, as things hadn't turned nasty and no blood was spilled . . .

I only hoped I had arrived in time.

Having checked that the coast was clear, I started up the left-hand gate. It was made from cast iron, intricately twirled and twisted, painted black – and easy to climb. I was up past the ornately curlicued 'G' at the top and down the other side in seconds. I paused for a moment, listening for the bark of a guard dog . . .

There was nothing.

To one side of the gates, the gatekeeper's lodge was in a terrible state. The door had been kicked in and was hanging off its hinges, and the windows had all been broken. I stepped inside. It was pitch-black. I reached inside my waistcoat pocket and drew out a box of Vestas. Striking a match, I held up the flickering flame and looked around.

Obviously someone had had it in for the Major. The place had been ransacked. Curtains had been pulled from the windows; pictures torn from the wall and dashed to the floor. An old leather armchair was on its side, its stuffing spilling out like the entrails of a butchered ox, and an oak table had been reduced to matchwood.

I stepped back outside, remembering the wild, haunted expression in the eyes of the gatekeeper. Poor honest fellow, I thought. He had obviously refused to go along with the headmaster and his cronies, and had suffered grievously as a result. By the look of things, he'd only just escaped with his life – though in the event, of course, that had tragically proved to be only a temporary reprieve.

As I struck a second match, I caught sight of something at my feet. It was a large tasselled feather. Bright emerald, with wispy tips. I stooped down and picked it up.

The headmaster's precious stuffed birds, I thought with contempt as I examined the feather. Those horrible dead things seemed to mean more to him than living, breathing flesh and blood.

I glanced back at the wrecked gatehouse. As lock-ups went, this looked like a bad one. There was evil about. I could sense it. Gripping the handle of my swordstick, I turned my back on the lodge and headed across the playing fields towards the brightly lit main buildings of the school.

They were, I had to concede, magnificent – a fact which made the change in the school's circumstances all the more unfortunate. The broad sweep of the east and west wings met at the grand central portico with its four stucco columns beneath a Grecian pediment. Through the portico lay the central court-yard, or quadrangle, from which, as I crept closer, I could hear voices.

Instinctively, I dropped to my haunches. I removed my coalstack hat, clicking it flat and stowing it in my topcoat. My right thumb flicked the catch on my swordstick as, out there in the middle of the playing fields, I crouched down in the inky darkness and waited.

The voices grew louder, buzzing and monotonous like the droning of angry bees, combining into an insistent chant.

'Hunt the hog! Hunt the hog!'

All at once there was a loud whooping cheer from the quadrangle, followed a moment later by an agonized, high-pitched wail of terror.

What in hell's fiery furnace was going on? I asked myself as my muscles tensed in the darkness.

I didn't have to wait long to find out.

Suddenly a lone figure burst through the columns of the portico and out onto the playing field, running as fast as his legs would take him. Behind him, screeching and hooting like a horde of demented demons, came a pursuing mob.

Some carried blazing torches aloft, the yellow flames bathing the whole seething mass in a pool of flickering light. Some brandished bats and clubs; some wielded splintered table legs and bits of broken desks. A couple wore ornate feathered head-dresses. Several had blankets and curtains wrapped round their shoulders like cloaks. All were intent on running their quarry to ground.

The figure, sobbing and whimpering with terror, plunged into the darkness of the playing fields, and I drew back as he lumbered

Screeching and hooting like a horde of demented demons . . .

towards me. All at once, with a muddy squelch, he stumbled and fell, sprawling headlong on the turf. I stepped forward and, gripping him by the arm, hauled him to his feet. He turned his mud-smeared face to mine, his eyes wide with terror.

It was the games master, Mr Cripps.

His cracked lips opened. 'Help me,' he pleaded, his voice little more than a rasping whisper. 'Help . . . me . . .'

'Hunt the hog! Hunt the hog!'

The fiendish cries of the pursuing mob jolted Cripps back into action. He pushed past me and headed off into the blackness in the direction of the school gates and the promise of escape. His pursuers followed close behind. I dropped to my knees once more, cloaking myself in darkness as they swept past.

I felt the heat from the blazing torches and smelled the burning pitch. I saw the blur of brandished weapons, and heard the yelp and shriek of voices that seemed barely human.

One figure, wrapped in a length of striped curtain, dropped the sharpened stump of a chair leg and crouched to retrieve it from the mud. The curtain fell from his shoulders. I recognized at once that round, red-cheeked face, the tousle-haired head . . .

'Sidney junior,' I muttered under my breath.

The next instant, he seized the chair leg and was off once more with the others, baying at the top of his voice. I thought of his father reading the lock-up letter, and wondered what 'the proudest father in the whole world' would have to say if he could see his son now.

'Please! Please! Please!' I heard the abject cries of the games master echoing back across the field above the howls of glee from his pursuers. The hunt had obviously run its victim to ground.

Keeping to the darkness beyond the

flickering torchlight, I approached as close as I dared. After the seeming chaos of the chase, the hunters were now working calmly and methodically. I saw the gleam of leather and a momentary flash of metal, bright in the moonlight, as one school belt was fastened around Cripps's neck, another around his waist, and the two fastened together. As they worked, the individual screeches and cries subsided, and a new chant was taken up.

'Bring him to the head! Bring him to the head!'

It was low and hypnotic, and I realized that everyone was responding to its rhythm. Those binding the games teacher were doing it at the same pace, while those watching were swaying from side to side like metronomes. The only one not following the same mesmeric beat was Cripps himself, who tugged and struggled at every opportunity, desperate still to break free – not that it did him a ha'p'orth of good.

Softly at first, though soon rising in volume, the new chant caught on.

'Bring him to the head! Bring him to the head! Bring him to the head!'

'No!' Cripps cried out. 'No, for the love of all that is sacred, not that! Let me go, I beg you! Let me go!'

No one paid him any heed as they tugged him to his feet. Even though his voice grew louder and louder until he was screaming hysterically, it was drowned out by the rising swell of the chanting.

'Bring him to the head! Bring him to the head!'

What manner of evil was the headmaster orchestrating in this lock-up academy? I wondered as the mob approached.

As they had been swaying, so now they were marching, each individual in the hunting party in step with the others as they strode back across the fields to the rhythm of the echoing chant. In their midst, struggling no longer, was Mr Cripps. He was walking along so obediently, his head down and his eyes to the ground, that no one needed to tug on the leashes that bound him any longer.

The victorious hunting pack marched past me in the darkness. As it did so, I picked up the length of curtain that young Sidney junior had dropped, wrapped it round my shoulders, and fell into step at the back of the throng. Ahead of me, the chant continued.

'Bring him to the head! Bring him to the head!'

The sense of evil I'd felt from the moment I'd scaled the gates of Grassington Hall gripped me more powerfully than ever. I thought of the beautiful Mei Ling waiting for me to show up for my usual yinchido lesson. How far away the laundry now seemed as I followed the chanting crowd into the school.

From the top of my head to the marrow in

my bones, I knew that something terrible was about to unfold in this place. As to what it was, I could only guess, yet as I stepped through the portico and into the quadrangle, I knew I had to find out.

CHAPTER 9

'*B*ring him to the head! Bring him to the head!'

The voice of the mob echoed round the quadrangle as the boys clattered over the paving stones – with yours truly bringing up the rear, wrapped in the bedraggled curtain, trying to look inconspicuous. Not that I had to try very hard. The pupils seemed far too preoccupied with dragging and goading the games master in their midst to notice me.

At the far side of the quad, beyond the central fountain, a great tongue of yellow lamplight poured out from the main entrance of the school and across the paving stones.

The mob and their prisoner funnelled in through the arched doorway. I went with them.

I'd seen lock-up academies where masters imprisoned their pupils and I'd seen school rebellions where the pupils resisted the masters. But this was different from both. The school gates were certainly locked, but inside, it was the pupils who seemed to have the upper hand. But then again, if the chants were to be believed, the headmaster was still in charge.

It didn't make any sense.

As the pupils crowded into the hallway, I found myself being jostled and shoved in the middle of a great milling crowd, and I lost sight of Mr Cripps. Peering over the sea of bobbing heads, I noticed older boys dressed in curious feathered head-dresses directing the others.

'Heron House!' one of them shouted, his voice shrill yet authoritative. 'To your dorms.

Eagle House on guard duty . . .'

It was Thompson, the boy who'd been injured on the Farrow Fives field – although in his emerald feathered head-dress and paint-daubed face, he looked as if he belonged in a jungle rather than a school. With his jaw grimly set and his eyes blazing, he thrust his arm out and pointed along the corridor.

'Falcon House, bring the prisoner to the head!'

Ahead of me, the surging crowd began to split up and set off in different directions, with the boys around what I took to be the hunched figure of Mr Cripps heading off down the corridor in the direction of the headmaster's study.

'To the head! To the head!' they chanted urgently, their voices all but drowning out the anguished cries of the hapless games master.

I had to think quickly. Here in the middle of the rapidly emptying entrance hall I was about to stand out like a carpenter's thumb, curtain or no curtain. Glancing to my left, I spotted the figure of Sidney junior heading up the stairs with, presumably, other members of Heron House. Perhaps he could shed some light on the matter, I thought as I fell into step behind him.

At the top of the staircase I found myself making my way along a wide hallway, before tramping up some more stairs to a second, narrower corridor lit by flickering gas lamps. We traipsed along it in single file, our footsteps echoing. There were doors leading off it on both sides, each one with a number on the central panel, and as pupils reached their own dormitory, they broke ranks and entered.

I stuck close behind the sloping shoulders of the coal merchant's son. As he turned left into Dormitory 12, I followed him.

Up in the roof, the unlit dorm was long and narrow, with small, barred windows set into the sloping ceiling. Twelve beds were squashed into the wedge-shaped space, six on one side of the room and six on the other. The place had probably been spick and span once – cosy, even. But not any longer. The floor was strewn with bedclothes and blankets, and across every surface was a fine covering of feathery down, spilled from the torn pillows.

Sidney – shuffling now with the weary gait of a sleepwalker – made his way across the floor and sat down heavily at the end of his low iron-framed bed. I went with him and sat on the adjacent bed. I looked at him. In the dim light from the corridor I could see that his face looked pale and drawn. The events of that night had evidently taken their toll.

'Sidney,' I said. He looked up, an expression of confusion passing across his podgy features as his eyes met mine. 'Sidney, it's Barnaby Grimes. From your father's coalyard. Remember?'

'Father,' he whispered softly. 'Father ...' Tears welled up in his eyes.

'Sidney,' I persisted, 'what's going on? What were you doing out there on the playing fields ... ?'

'What the head told us to do,' he said, his voice low and emotionless as his unblinking eyes stared into midair.

'The headmaster *told* you to hunt the games master?' I said. 'But why?'

'Because the head told us to,' he said firmly.

I thought of my own encounters with Archimedes Barnett. He'd seemed so affable, so avuncular, with the best interests of the boys uppermost in his thoughts.

How wrong could I have been?

'Sidney,' I said, pushing the ragged curtain aside and reaching into a pocket of my waistcoat for a pencil and notebook, 'you must write a note to your father. Tell him what's going on here. I'll deliver it personally—'

Just then, there was a cry of 'Lights out!' from outside. As the lamps in the corridor were abruptly extinguished, the dormitory was plunged into darkness. Around me there was the rustling of blankets and the creaking of bed-springs as the occupants of Dormitory 12 clambered into their beds in the pitch-black.

Strangely for a school dorm, there was none of the usual whispered conversation or furtive sniggering that accompanied lights out. Just an unearthly silence, which was followed soon after by quiet, rhythmic breathing. If I tried stumbling around in this inky blackness, I realized with an inward groan, I ran the risk of clattering into all manner of things, making a terrible racket and drawing attention to myself – and most likely breaking my neck in the process.

Sidney's letter would have to wait. There was nothing for it but to bed down and wait for the cold light of dawn. Pulling my curtain around me, I sat down, propped myself up against the wall between the beds of Sidney and his neighbour – and waited.

I must have dozed off, for the next thing I remember was a voice in my ear, soft and insidious.

'Arise, my children,' it said. 'Arise and prepare.'

I opened my eyes. Early morning light was streaming in through the barred windows. I looked around, expecting someone to be there – a prefect, perhaps, or one of the teachers. But there was no one.

'Arise, my children,' the voice continued. 'Arise and prepare.'

I clearly wasn't the only one to have heard it. Around me, the other boys in the dormitory had climbed from their beds, wiped the sleep from their eyes and were already beginning to file out through the door. I turned to young Sidney, hoping that at last we would be able to get that letter written alerting Sidney senior to his son's plight.

No such luck. The kid was already up and padding obediently after the others across the dormitory floor.

'Sidney,' I hissed. 'Sidney . . .'

I might as well have been talking to myself. I seized him by the shoulders, but he shrugged me off like a barge dog shaking off canal water.

Reluctantly I followed Sidney and my dormitory companions back along the corridor and down the stairs. I was hungry – my stomach grumbling louder than a washerwoman on a wet Monday. But when we reached the bottom of the stairs, there was no sign of breakfast and the prefects ushered us towards the classrooms.

'Fall in, Heron House!' they bellowed, their words echoing along the corridor.

Most of them were wearing feathered head-dresses while, curiously, others were dressed in schoolmasters' clothes – white laboratory coats, leather-patched tweed jackets, mortar boards and flapping gowns. All of them were armed. Beneath my curtain cloak, I gripped my swordstick and kept my head down.

'Falcon House to the west classrooms! Heron House to the quad!'

I trooped after Sidney junior and his pals as they made their way towards the quad, past the line of supervising prefects in their feathered head-dresses. I was just approaching the last in line when he leaned forward, grabbed my arm and pulled me towards him. It was Thompson – but changed. He was no longer the eager guide who had shown me to the headmaster's study on my first visit. Now, his face was hard, his eyes glazed and his jaw fiercely clenched.

'Who are you?' he demanded. 'I don't recognize your face.'

'Me?' I said, coolly holding his gaze.

'I'm Grimes. Grimes minor.'

His eyes continued to bore into mine.

'I once substituted for you on the Farrow Fives field,' I told him.

I saw a flash of recognition, or memory, pass across his frowning features. He let me go, but I knew he remained suspicious. Setting off once again, I felt his piercing gaze on my back as I made my way out into the quad.

I discovered that we were heading towards the west wing. There were classrooms on both the ground and first floors, with doors leading out either onto a raised balcony or onto the quad itself. The ornate guttering with its gurning gargoyles, the brass and stone statues guarding each entrance, and the rose and ivy winding their way round each window, made it a building worthy of a stately home. As I drew nearer, though, the sounds of banging and crashing and splintering of wood reminded me all too clearly that this was no duke's palace, but rather a school in turmoil.

All at once a huge cupboard landed heavily on the paving stones to my left with a loud *crash!* A derisory cheer went up from above me and I looked up to see half a dozen boys standing on an upper balcony, looking down, grinning. A moment later, there was another loud whoop as a blackboard was hurled from the adjacent balcony and struck the ground with a splintering *crunch!*

Soon the air was thick with flying wood, as chairs, benches and desks, wardrobes and wainscoting, and even floorboards were torn from the classrooms both upstairs and down, and tossed unceremoniously out into the quadrangle. For a moment the boys in the quad waited.

'*Build,*' came the insidious voice, close by my ear.

Around me, the boys of Heron House began picking up cracked, damaged and broken pieces of furniture and lugging them off to the centre of the quad.

'*Build*,' the voice insisted.

To my surprise, I found myself joining in the feverish work. Back and forth I went, working with the other boys, shifting broken desks and splintered benches to the middle of the quadrangle, and helping to build them up into a tall structure. With my highstacking skills, it was easy for me to climb up the growing pile – nudging this broken door across, sliding that splintered chair leg into place – ensuring that the emerging pyramid grew both tall and stable.

'*Higher*,' the voice urged us on. '*Higher*.'

It was only when I was returning for more broken wood, and happened to glance up and notice a face in a window opposite, that I was jolted back to my senses. The face was that of a late-middle-aged man. He was stooped, sunken-cheeked and wild-eyed – but clearly a schoolmaster of some sort.

'Higher,' the voice urged us on. 'Higher.'

The next moment, he was abruptly gone . . .

That must be the teachers' common room, I thought. Perhaps the schoolmaster and his colleagues could provide me with some answers. I decided to pay them a visit.

Affecting a casual stroll and checking over my shoulder, I slipped away. I went round the side of the west wing, keeping to the shadows. At the end of the building I discovered a rough stone wall, which I scaled, the surface scuffing my knees and grazing my hands. With a groan of effort, I pulled myself onto a pitched roof above. I was hoping for a skylight, and was disappointed to find myself confronted with an unbroken vista of slate.

Undeterred, I crossed the parapet, made my way over the top of the central ridge-tiles and down the other side. From there, I was able to shin down an ornately decorated drainpipe – unsteady and swaying – until I found a small upper window that had been left ajar.

With a final effort, I hauled myself in, and found myself in a small and, by the look of all the dust and cobwebs, seldom used stock-room. I cautiously unlatched and pushed the door in front of me. It opened onto a central corridor. I peered out and looked in one direction, then the other.

'Which way?' I murmured.

And then I saw it – a gold-painted plaque on the door opposite. MASTERS' COMMON ROOM, I read. I'd struck lucky.

Checking again that the coast was clear, I darted across to the door and tried the handle. It was locked. Somehow I wasn't surprised. I removed a skeleton key from the fourth pocket of my waistcoat, and gingerly inserted it in the lock.

From my left I heard voices. One of them sounded like Thompson's. I froze. To my relief, a moment later they all faded away.

Click.

The lock gave. I turned the handle, pushed open the door and walked into the room. Inside, tied hand and foot, were twenty schoolmasters sitting stiffly on the floor, surrounded by the shattered debris of what had once been finely upholstered armchairs and side tables. It was as if a hurricane had hit the first-class salon of an ocean liner and I was looking at the shipwrecked survivors.

They turned wide, staring eyes towards me – eyes filled with fear and trepidation, rather than any hope of rescue.

'It's all right,' I tried to reassure them, sweeping back my curtain disguise and revealing my waistcoat and swordstick. 'I'm an outsider. I'm not from the school.' I looked from one to the other. 'Can any of you tell me what's going on here . . . ?'

I stopped, for I'd suddenly noticed, lying at my feet and staring up at me with unseeing eyes, small whimpering sounds escaping from his cracked lips, the mud-caked games master, Mr Cripps.

'W-what happened to him?' I asked.

The tall, hook-nosed master whose face I'd glimpsed at the window stared at me. 'He tried to escape,' he said, swallowing anxiously. 'They . . . they . . . took him to see the head.'

CHAPTER 10

As I stared down at the games master, a mere husk of his former self, his body drained and his mind destroyed, I heard sounds from the other side of the common-room door. Tramping footsteps and voices, getting rapidly louder as they approached along the corridor.

'Follow me, Falcon House, proceed!'

The barked command came from right outside the door of the masters' common room. I'd been careless. I'd unlocked the door with a skeleton key – and left it unlocked. The discovery was bound to give me away.

I leaped forward, pulled the key from my

waistcoat pocket and slipped it into the lock.

'Give me the keys, Simmonds major.'

My heart hammered in my chest. The prefect's voice was inches away. Only the thin panel of wood separated us.

At the sound of his command, there was a jangling of keys on a key chain. I turned my key quickly, hoping no one would hear the telltale click, and removed it – and not a moment too soon. An instant later, the prefect in the corridor thrust his own key into the lock and turned . . .

Leaping back from the door, I ducked down behind an upturned armchair beside the window. The next moment, the door flew open, slamming against the wall with a thunderous *crash!*

'All of you, up!' barked one of the prefects. 'The head has work for you.'

'Now!' shouted a second, and from my hiding place I heard the sound of a heavy implement – a makeshift bludgeon or a home-made studded club – hammering against a cupboard, splintering the wood.

There were sighs and groans as the bound masters struggled awkwardly to their feet. One of them muttered something under his breath.

'And no talking!' bellowed the first prefect. 'Take them to the bird hall.'

There was more clomping of feet as the boys trooped into the room.

'What about him?' someone asked.

'What, Cripps?' the prefect said. 'Leave him. He won't be going anywhere.'

The boys laughed unpleasantly. I found their indifference to the master's suffering deeply shocking.

'You lot! Get a move on!' the prefect's voice sounded again. 'The head is getting impatient!'

As the footsteps and voices retreated, I stole a glance from behind the wrecked armchair. The last couple of teachers – both of them escorted on either side by boys who were prodding them viciously with their makeshift weapons – were disappearing through the door. A tall prefect with red hair and a blue feathered head-dress, who was bringing up the rear, reached out and grabbed the door handle.

Seconds later, the door slammed shut. I waited a moment, then emerged from behind the armchair, to see Mr Cripps sitting on the floor and staring out of the window, his eyes lifeless, his gaze unblinking. It was unlikely that he'd noticed a single thing that had just happened.

'Here,' I said gently as I poured him a cup of water from a chipped pitcher. 'Drink this.'

He neither heard me nor saw me, and when I put the cup to his cracked lips, the water simply trickled down over his chin. It was hopeless. The master was like one of those stuffed birds I'd seen earlier – hollow, lifeless . . . There was nothing I could do for him.

I shuddered. I doubted there was anything *anyone* could do for him.

The masters had been taken to the bird hall and I intended to follow them, but at a safe distance. I, for one, had no intention of being sent to the headmaster. Gripping the handle of my swordstick tightly, I set off along the corridor.

I heard the footsteps retreating, and the sound of the masters' protestations and appeals fading away.

'Please, Ridley,' beseeched one. 'Stop this madness. You're a good lad at heart . . .'

'Morrison!' came another. 'It's not too late. Release us, and we can talk about it . . .'

At the end of the hallway I glanced through a large window. Outside, in the quad, the boys of Heron and Eagle houses were working on the pyramid of wrecked furniture.

And what a pyramid it was!

Its four sides consisted of a series of rough steps, rising to a flat platform at the top, almost as high as the roofline of the quad. The surrounding classrooms must have been stripped bare to construct this massive pile.

Ahead of me, the crocodile line of teachers was being led up a separate staircase – one that, from my previous visit, I knew went to the headmaster's bird hall. The prefects beat their cudgels and bellowed at the hapless masters, who were still pleading to be freed.

'The head says, "No talking!" Hurry, time is short!'

Just then, from behind me, I heard a noise that made my heart jump into my mouth. I spun round, my hand gripping my sword-stick beneath my curtain cape, to find myself staring at a rather hot and sticky-looking Sidney junior. He was struggling up the stairs with a carpet bag under one arm and a wickerwork basket under the other.

'Give me a hand,' he wheezed breathlessly, shoving the wicker basket into my hands.

I took it and followed Sidney, who was redder than ever from his recent exertions in the quad, his flaxen hair plastered to his temples with sweat.

'What is this?' I asked.

He frowned. 'Matron's sewing basket, of course,' he panted. 'The head wants it in the bird hall. Immediately. And this' – he held up the carpet bag – 'is the rest of her yarn. Come on! We've got to hurry, the head says . . .'

I followed him along the corridor, past the big window, round to the left and up the staircase towards the bird hall. I remembered the last time I'd been here. The headmaster had been insistent that no boys were allowed in there unsupervised – yet there were Sidney and I, making our way up the stairs on his express orders.

Nothing about this school rebellion made sense.

The route to the bird hall bore all the scars of the chaos and destruction that had afflicted the rest of the school. The carpet had been torn from the floor; the pictures on the walls had been smashed to smithereens. As for the door to the hall itself, the wood around the handle was a mass of jagged splinters, where the lock had been smashed in.

Sidney knocked. The broken door opened with a creak, and Thompson stood there, hands on his hips and an impatient expression on his face.

'The head said to hurry,' he said. 'Time is short.'

'I came as fast as I could . . .' Sidney began, tears springing to his eyes.

Ignoring him, Thompson pointed across the room.

If the corridor had been damaged by the unruly pupils of Grassington Hall, then the headmaster's beloved bird hall had been all but destroyed. Without exception, the glass in each and every one of the display cabinets had been smashed, and now lay on the floor like the shattered surface of a frozen lake, which crunched underfoot as we stepped inside.

'Put them down over there!' Thompson commanded, pointing towards the window at the far end of the long, thin gallery.

We did as we were told. I kept my head down and my curtain cape pulled close round me as I took the opportunity to glance furtively around.

Inside the broken cabinets were the masters, seated upon the floor. Before them lay a pile of birds, wrenched from their mounts; beside them were sacks full of feathers. Each of the birds, which had been so lovingly stuffed, named and mounted in a setting that matched its origins, was now being systematically plucked.

The master nearest to me was sitting in a jungle scene, tugging the feathers from a green and red parrot. His crouching neighbour was plucking a duck. The hook-nosed teacher I'd spoken to earlier squatted in a beige and khaki savannah, his head down as he yanked out the salmon-pink feathers of a giant flamingo with the single-minded determination of a man possessed.

' "Faster!" the head says. "Faster!" ' urged the red-haired prefect, striding between the stooped heads of the masters, brandishing a cane.

Even as he spoke, I heard a voice close by my ear. *'Faster, my children,'* it whispered urgently. *'Work faster!'*

As if in answer, the red-haired prefect rained a series of savage blows down on the shoulders of the hapless masters, who groaned and whimpered pitifully. I felt the blood rush to my face, and took a step towards the bully, only to feel a hand on my shoulder.

'You! Grimes minor, isn't it?'

I turned to see Thompson eyeing me

suspiciously. 'Gather the feathers and take them to the cloak maker.'

He nodded across the hall. I followed his gaze.

There, at the centre of the chaos, a small fair-haired pupil in wire-framed spectacles and an over-sized apron festooned with needles of all shapes and sizes was busily working on what looked at first sight to be a great carpet of feathers.

I stooped and picked up a sack of exotic feathers, recently plucked from what had once been a pink-kneed stork from the Ocavandia Wetlands, according to the label on the case. Brushing past Thompson, I made my way across the broken glass to the diminutive carpet weaver.

As I stood over the little fellow, whose nimble fingers darted back and forth in a blur of movement, I could see that it wasn't a carpet he was working on after all. In fact, dashing backward and forward like a crazed

Working on what looked at first sight to be a great carpet of feathers.

woodpecker, he was sewing feathers onto roughly cut squares of some dark material – formerly stage curtains by the look of them.

There were twelve in all, and the boy was working at phenomenal speed, like someone possessed. I dumped my sack next to him, and he grasped a handful and continued sewing without looking up. I watched, mesmerized, as he reached the bottom of the twelfth square, only to dart back to the first, to begin stitching another layer of feathers.

What on earth could this frenzy of activity be for? I wondered.

Just then, a loud bugle call sounded, echoing up the stairs from the hallway. Around me, a loud baying went up as the boys raised their heads and howled.

Sidney appeared at my elbow, licking his lips. 'Food!' he grinned.

I suddenly realized how hungry I was. The last thing I'd eaten was a Stover's Special, and that more than twenty-four hours earlier.

I was so hungry I could have eaten a drayman's horse in full harness – *and* the cart as well . . .

The prefects sprang into action, shouting commands. Three boys were told to gather up the feathered squares and take them downstairs. A dozen more – along with two of the prefects – were charged with returning the masters to their common room. The rest of us were instructed to make our way down to the dining hall.

'The head says, "Feast!" You have done well!' the red-haired prefect called after us.

Down the stairs I went, amid a surge of whooping and yelling schoolboys, all evidently as hungry as I was. The doors of the dining hall were thrown open at our approach and, pushing and shoving in the crush, I found myself in a huge dark room with wooden panels on the walls and heavy beams spanning the vaulted ceiling high above my head – though completely emptied of all benches and tables.

Presumably, I thought, the furniture had all been smashed up with the rest to be used to build the great pyramid outside.

As more boys arrived, the noise in the hall grew. Howling, barking, yelping and snarling, they sounded more like a pack of starving hounds than a hall of hungry schoolboys. Suddenly the doors at the far end were thrown open. Inside the hall, the crowd fell back, leaving an aisle which led from the entrance to the centre of the floor. All around me, the baying boys pulled out short, sharp knives from their belts, and raised them into the air, while their cries became blood-chilling screams.

A moment later, half a dozen older, athletic-looking boys appeared in the doorway. They seemed to be carrying something between them on their shoulders.

All at once – as they stepped forward – a hush descended over the dining hall as each and every boy held his breath. You could have heard a feather drop. The six boys made their way across the hall, and as they drew closer, I peered over the bobbing heads of my companions.

With a sharp intake of breath, I saw that resting upon their shoulders was the body of a slaughtered deer, its head lolling to one side and blood dripping down onto the floor from a vicious wound in its neck, from which two feathered arrows emerged. When they reached the centre of the dining hall, they eased the carcass off their shoulders with a grunt and stood back as it fell to the floor with a dull thud.

As I looked down, I heard a voice close to my ear whisper, '*Feast, my children. Feast.*'

The next moment, the silence of the great dining hall was shattered by the sound of two hundred voices, high-pitched and screaming, baying for blood. All around me the boys surged forward, their knives raised. They fell upon the carcass like wild beasts, and began tearing and hacking at it with their knives, nails and teeth. Strips of raw flesh were ripped from the still-warm body of the deer, and the floor became slippery with blood as the boys fought to get close enough to grab a morsel.

I staggered backward as they surged forward, howling and screaming. Those who had already cut off flesh of their own allowed themselves to be shoved aside. They retreated to the corners, guarding the chunks of raw meat against anyone who came too close with snarls and growls and slashes of their blades – to be replaced by others, fresh to the slaughtered body, who buried their faces in the bloody carcass and hacked off chunks of meat of their own.

Extricating myself from this sickening mob, I made my way to the back of the hall. My head was spinning; my brow was wet and clammy. I was badly shaken, and I needed a moment to think.

Abandoning any thought of extracting a letter from Sidney, or anyone else, I knew that I had to escape from Grassington Hall and alert the authorities to this horror without delay. I slunk away cautiously, glancing back over my shoulder to ensure I wasn't being followed, and was making my way towards the gatehouse when something suddenly occurred to me.

The masters were still locked up inside their common room.

I couldn't leave them there. Not with the madness infecting the school. If the boys had been capable of slaughtering and devouring a deer, what might they do to their hapless masters?

Turning on my heel, I sped back the way I'd come. I leaped in through a broken ground-floor window, dashed across the ruins of a devastated science laboratory and up the stairs on the other side. From somewhere behind me, echoing loudly, I could hear the shrieks and howls of the bloodthirsty mob of boys, still tearing into their bloody feast. Along the upper corridor I went until I came to the door of the masters' common room again.

It was only when I reached into the pocket of my waistcoat for the skeleton key that I realized just how much my hands were shaking. Suddenly all fingers and thumbs, I managed to pull the key free – breathing deeply in an attempt to calm my shattered nerves – and inserted it into the lock. From inside, I heard the sound of voices, suddenly raised in panic.

'It's all right,' I murmured. 'It's me, Barnaby Grimes . . .'

I was just about to turn the key when a voice hissed menacingly behind me.

'Grimes minor, I might have known . . .'

CHAPTER 11

I spun round, to be confronted by Thompson in his emerald feathered head-dress, a heavy fives bat clutched in both hands. Behind him, the eleven other prefects – each one similarly head-dressed and armed – glowered at me like country kestrels eyeing a town pigeon.

'Grimes minor,' Thompson snarled. 'I've had my eye on you from the start . . .'

'I can explain,' I began, playing for time while I sized up the odds.

They didn't look good. One of me and twelve of them. I didn't stand a chance in a fair fight. I fingered my swordstick beneath my cape – knowing what terrible damage I could do with its blade.

But no. I couldn't shed blood. Whatever had got into them, they were still just schoolboys after all. There had to be another way . . .

'I was just passing,' I said, 'when I heard a commotion inside. I thought the masters might be trying to escape, so I thought I ought to check—'

'*Seize him!*' a voice hissed, close by my ear.

The next instant, Thompson and his mates threw themselves at me like out-fielders in a Farrow Fives match. They were quick, but I was quicker. I hadn't studied the ancient art of yinchido with my beautiful teacher, Mei Ling, all summer for nothing. Now 'The Way of the Silver Mist' came to my rescue.

I leaped to my right, through the gap between Thompson and the big red-haired prefect at his shoulder. Dropping to my knees, I upended a tall, solidly built lad in a crimson head-dress coming up behind me, and roughly shoulder-barged two more as I slid clear on my knees.

The next moment, I was back on my feet, racing down the corridor with the feathered prefects snapping at my heels like a flock of enraged peacocks. I took a left turn, then a right – the sounds of footsteps behind me echoing down the bare corridors. I was heading for the staircase that led down to the entrance hall.

If I can just make it out into the quad, I might stand a chance, I told myself . . .

Turning the next corner, I slammed on the brakes. The prefects had obviously split up. Six were still behind me. But the rest – led by Thompson – had doubled back, and now appeared ahead of me on the landing, blocking my escape.

I was surrounded!

I fingered the catch on my swordstick. It

would have been so easy to flick it back and unsheathe the blade . . .

No! I once again reminded myself sharply. These are schoolboys. I can't hurt them!

'*Seize him*!' the voice hissed.

In front of me, three prefects closed in, their mallets swinging in classic ankle-height scything sweeps, while three stayed behind to cover their backs. Mr Cripps had coached his fives team well, I thought, with bitter irony. Behind me, I sensed three more bat-wielding prefects approaching.

One . . . two . . . three . . . I counted off the beats in my head. *Now!*

I leaped high in the air, my legs raised up beneath me, swinging my swordstick in a broad shoulder-height sweep as I did so. Below me, six prefects scythed each other's ankles out from under one another, while my swordstick clattered against their heads. Down they went, like painted skittles in a fairground sideshow, as I landed on my feet and backed against the balustrade that ran the length of the landing.

Below, in the entrance hall, boys were emerging from their gruesome feast and raising inquisitive, blood-stained faces towards the commotion at the top of the stairs. In front of me, Thompson and the five remaining prefects stepped over their groaning colleagues and closed in for the kill.

'Look, I don't want to fight you,' I pleaded. 'Let me go before it's too late and someone gets badly hurt . . .'

I might as well have been talking to myself for all the notice Thompson and his chums took of my words. Their faces were mask-like, their eyes as dead and expressionless as if set in marble statues.

The red-haired prefect swung his bat viciously at my head from the left, while two others attacked from the right, their mallets at shin height. I jumped back out of the way of Ginger's blow, jutting out an elbow that caught him full in the throat, while kicking out at the two on my right. The heel of my boot slammed into two faces, one after the other – and all three prefects went down on their knees, gurgling and gasping for breath as I landed back on my feet. Behind him, Thompson's two remaining companions hesitated as I brandished my sheathed sword-stick at them in desperation.

'It's not too late—' I began.

Suddenly, with a guttural, animal-like roar of rage, Thompson threw himself at me, his face contorted into a mask of pure hate. Instinctively, I sidestepped and ducked, falling to my knees as I did so.

Thompson – arms flailing and unable to stop himself – shot past me and over the balustrade, into the great gaping void of the entrance hall. Stomach pitching, I peered after him, through the spindles of the balustrade, just in time to see a look of startled

Suddenly, with a guttural, animal-like roar of rage, Thompson threw himself at me . . .

panic flash across his face as he fell.

Moments later, there was a sickening crunch, and I forced myself to look down. There, on the marble floor of the entrance hall, lay Thompson's broken body – arms twisted, legs bent, his head surrounded by a spreading halo of dark red blood.

Too late, behind me, I heard the telltale whistling sound of a fives bat swinging through the air, and felt a heavy blow strike me hard on the back of the head. There was an instant of shock and pain.

Then nothing . . .

When I regained my senses, I was being dragged by my legs unceremoniously down the stairs by two prefects. My hands were roughly tied, my swordstick was gone and my head thudded painfully against each step as we descended. Down in the entrance hall I was bundled to my feet and led past poor Thompson, who still lay like a broken marionette in a pool of blood.

Perhaps the most chilling thing about the gruesome scene was the casual indifference to his body shown by the boys milling around. Something was very wrong here in Grassington Hall, I told myself as the prefects dragged me down a wood-panelled corridor. There was an evil infecting the place, turning these boys into savage beasts, immune to suffering.

But who was responsible?

We came to a halt. I looked up at the plaque screwed into the dark wood panels of the door – a single word, spelled out in intricate gold letters.

HEADMASTER

The door opened slowly and the prefects pushed me roughly in the back, sending me stumbling inside. The door creaked closed behind me. I seemed to be alone in the

gloom of the headmaster's study.

The first thing that struck me was the smell. It was a curious heady odour, like a mixture of formaldehyde and snuffed candles, which caught in my throat and made me light-headed. It appeared to be emanating from the single source of light, a smoking oil lamp which stood in the centre of the headmaster's desk beside an inkpot and a tattered quill. The meagre glow it gave off was muted and orange, and seemed almost to cast more shadow than it did light.

Behind the desk was a high leather wingback chair, turned towards the wall, on which the headmaster's qualifications hung in gilt frames. The glass was cracked and the certificates were torn and defaced – but I could still make out the crest of one of the older universities, and the letters following the headmaster's name.

Archimedes Barnett, BA (Hons), MA, MRSA.

As I squinted at the certificates, the leather chair slowly turned to reveal the slumped shape of the headmaster himself, hideously transformed. His clothes were stained with blood and, in places, ripped to shreds, as if slashed by the claws of some vicious bird of prey. His cheeks were sunken, his hair matted and lank, while his skin was sallow, waxen and badly bruised.

His eyes stared into mine, deep-set, dark-ringed and full of torment. His spectacles were twisted, the lenses shattered, and hung down from one ear like some barbaric ornament. Not that it mattered, for Archimedes Barnett was staring right through me with haunted, unseeing eyes.

'What have I done? What have I done?' he muttered over and over again to himself, drool dribbling down from the corners of his mouth.

I don't believe he was even aware that I was in the room. Whatever caused the

shudders and twitches that now racked his body, it was a horror that only he could see.

'My children,' he murmured, his voice now little more than a defeated rasp. 'My children.' He twitched. 'My poor, poor children ...' Tears welled up in his eyes and rolled down his cheeks, leaving tracks like snail-trails down his grimy face. 'What have I done?'

'*Here,*' came a hissing voice, seemingly whispering close by my ear.

It was my turn to twitch, as I looked past the babbling headmaster towards the back of the study. There stood a second door.

Slowly it opened, as if by an invisible hand, to reveal a small inner chamber on the other side. It was the headmaster's private library, the walls clad with shelves laden with leather-bound books. The smell I'd noticed when I first entered the study became stronger than ever.

Despite myself, I stumbled towards the

open door and entered. On the wall facing me, both the shelves and the books had been removed, and now their torn and shredded remains formed a crude flat-topped pyramid – a miniature version of the great pyramid that the boys had constructed outside in the quad.

There were small candles flickering from each roughly hewn step of the pyramid's sides, and inkpots – now re-filled with some sour-smelling incense, whose smoke coiled up into the air and filled the study with an intoxicating fog. Around the base of the crude pyramid, the bones of what I took to be previous savage school dinners littered the floor: antlered skulls and jutting rib-cages.

But that is not what caught my eye. No, what made me gasp and shrink back instinctively was the thing at the top of the pyramid ... nestling upon a soft bed of exotic feathers ...

An emerald skull.

It was covered in slivers of a translucent green stone – jade, perhaps, or malachite – each one expertly cut and fixed into place. Every part of the skull – the jutting jaw, the jagged nasal socket, the grotesque ridges across the domed top, even the long teeth, fixed in a wicked parody of a grin – had been covered in the dazzling green veneer.

Extraordinary though the mosaic of the emerald skull was, it was nothing compared with its glittering eyes. Set deep into the skull's bony sockets were two huge blood-red rubies, cut into countless angled facets that twinkled and gleamed in the dancing candlelight as they stared back at me.

I couldn't take my eyes off that hideous crimson stare. I was transfixed. It was as though my strength was ebbing away. My legs felt weak, my breathing became harsh and laboured, and my chest tightened, as if an invisible fist was closing around my heart.

And, as I stared into them, the skull's ruby eyes began to glow with an inner fire, brighter and brighter, until they shone like two crimson rays directly into my eyes, filling my vision with a pulsating blood-red light. Then, whispering softly, came the voice.

'Fall to your knees before me, miserable slave. For it is I,' it hissed, *'the head.'*

CHAPTER

12

I will never forget the visions that filled my mind as I stared, transfixed, into the glowing red eyes of the emerald skull.

'*It is I, Catincatapetl, Emerald Messenger of Darkness, Master of the Underworld and Lord of Chaos. You belong to me . . .*'

The voice hissed in my head, each word laden with a dark and ancient evil.

I could see a verdant jungle, and a great stone pyramid rising out of it. I was surrounded by a vast crowd, murmuring, heads bowed, shuffling forward. I was being swept along with it towards the great pyramid and up its steps. The murmuring voices grew in intensity, rising to a crescendo as I approached the top.

'Catincatapetl! Catincatapetl!'

Overhead, the sky filled with dark, boiling clouds that spread across the horizon like a monstrous ink blot. I felt icy fingers tightening round my heart and a crushing weight bearing down on my chest so hard I could hardly breathe.

'Catincatapetl! Catincatapetl!'

The chant rose even higher to a deafening, screeching frenzy. Just as I felt that my head was about to explode, the chant stopped dead and, for an instant, the glowing eyes of the emerald skull flashed a dazzling brilliant white. There was a moment of intense, searing pain – as if my chest had been ripped open – and then a warm feathery darkness enveloped me, and all I could hear was the beat of a monstrous heart, drowning out all conscious thought.

Thud! Thud! Thud!

'Our hearts beat as one, child of Catincatapetl, servant of Darkness. Now, join the others.'

From that moment on, I was only dimly aware of my surroundings, and no longer questioned what I did or saw. It was as if I was in a dream; the only reality, the voice above the steady beating of the heart.

'Prepare the sacrifice, my children,' the voice hissed. 'The time draws near.'

As I stumbled down the corridor in a trance – the walls close up one moment, then telescoping endlessly away the next – other boys joined me. Their faces were daubed with paint. Crude weapons were clutched in their white-knuckled fists. Studded cudgels. Jointed flails. Blazing torches . . .

But none of this seemed strange to me now. It all made sense. We were one with Catincatapetl, the Emerald Messenger of Darkness. We all shared the one beating heart. The sound of chanting echoed up from the quad. The whole school was gathering outside, everyone taking up the same rhythmic cry.

'Catincatapetl! Catincatapetl . . .'

The chanted name ebbed and flowed, like music on the wind.

'*This way*,' the voice hissed inside my head, and I stepped out of the crowded corridor and through an open door to my left.

Abruptly the door slammed shut. I was in a cloakroom. Eleven prefects – dressed in feathered head-dresses of red, purple, yellow and black; feathered robes that rustled and hissed as they flapped, and grotesque beaked masks – turned towards me.

'*Robe yourself, my child*,' the voice commanded.

A pair of rough hands placed a head-dress on my head and tied a cape around my shoulders – hands which, with no sense of surprise, I realized were my own. I pulled the beaked mask over my face, and felt a strange surge of power and excitement as I did so. The heartbeat quickened imperceptibly.

'*Come, my condors!*' The voice sounded almost gleeful. '*The time is close upon us . . .*'

I fell into step behind the others as we marched in time to the heartbeat, out of the cloakroom and down the corridor towards the quad.

'Catincatapetl! Catincatapetl!'

The chanting reached a mesmeric fever-pitch as we emerged. The swaying multitude of boys bowed and scraped and stepped aside to let us pass. We strode between them, towards the great towering pyramid of wrecked furniture before us.

There was something strange about the air that we all seemed to sense, for a hush fell over the quad. Although the sun was high in the sky, there was an unnatural chill. I heard the distant sound of dogs barking, of sheep bleating and, although it was still mid-afternoon, great flocks of starlings and sparrows circled the sky as though looking for somewhere to roost for the night.

'*Approach, my condors,*' the voice commanded.

We climbed the steps of the pyramid, over shattered cabinets and splintered desks. Flaming torches flickered. Pots of incense gave off coils of smoke, at once acrid and aromatic. At the top, eleven battered and bedraggled masters cowered on the platform, bewildered and stupefied.

'*The time has come at last,*' the voice hissed. '*The time of darkness to be made eternal, my children . . .*'

The eleven feather-cloaked figures ahead of me fanned out across the platform.

'*For when twelve beating hearts are offered up to me by twelve innocents, my reign shall begin again. The sun will be extinguished and eternal darkness will cover the earth . . .*

Catincatapetl shall rule, my children!'

The heartbeat thumping in all our heads now quickened with excitement.

'Catincatapetl! Catincatapetl!' the schoolboys chanted from the quad below.

'Let he who was last among us be first to make the sacrifice!' the voice hissed.

The sky seemed to tense and tremble. The air abruptly cooled.

'Cut out his beating heart!' the ancient voice commanded, each syllable dripping with a dark evil that I was powerless to resist.

Overhead, the moon slid slowly but inexorably across the face of the sun, casting the courtyard into a dreadful silent dusk. And as the light faded, so did the last vestiges of my free will. There was nothing I could do. This was the total eclipse that my friend, PB, had been so excited about. I'd looked forward to it too – yet from where I stood now, it seemed like the harbinger of an appalling bloodbath.

A circle of shadowy figures clustered like a flock of hideous vultures around the great slab that lay before me. Their beaked faces and long rustling feathers quivered with awful anticipation as their dark eye-sockets turned, as one, towards me.

On awkward, stumbling legs I approached the wooden altar like a sleepwalker, climbing one step after the other, powerless to fight it.

The hideous figures parted as I drew closer. At the altar, I looked down. There, stripped to the waist, lying face up and spread-eagled, was the headmaster, roped into place. There were cuts and weals on his skin – some scabbed over, some fresh – and his ribs were sticking up, giving his chest the appearance of a damaged glockenspiel.

His head lolled to one side, and from his parted lips there came a low, rasping moan.

'Please,' he pleaded, gazing up at me with the panic-stricken eyes of a ferret-cornered rabbit. 'Don't do it, I'm begging you . . .'

At that moment the final dazzling rays of the sun were extinguished by the dark orb of the moon. The eclipse was complete. With dazed eyes, I looked up into the sky. The whole disc had turned pitch-black, and from the circumference of the circle a spiky ring of light streamed out in all directions, like a black merciless eye staring down from the heavens.

The tallest of the feathered figures stepped forward to face me. He wore a great crown of iridescent blue plumage. Behind him, nestling like a grotesque egg on the cushion of the headmaster's high-backed leather chair, was the hideous grinning skull. As I stared, the huge jewels in the skull's eye-sockets started to glow a bright and bloody crimson, which stained the eerie twilight of the eclipse.

The feathered figure reached into his cape and withdrew a large stone knife, which he held out to me. Again the ancient voice rasped in my head.

'*Cut out his beating heart!*'

Despite myself, I reached out and gripped the haft of the stone knife in my hands. As I did so, I felt my arm being raised up into the air, as if it was attached to a string tugged upwards by some unseen puppeteer.

I stared down at the headmaster, tied to the altar. A vivid cross of red paint marked the spot beneath which his heart lay, beating, I was sure, as violently as my own.

My grip tightened on the cruel stone knife, the blade glinting, as the blood-red ruby eyes of the grinning skull bored into mine. Inside my head, the voice rose to a piercing scream.

'*Cut out his beating heart – and give it to me!*'

I stepped towards the headmaster's mahogany desk, now transformed into a barbaric altar, flickering torchlight glinting on the flint blade. Before me, the headmaster whimpered pitifully – but I was indifferent to his plight. The head had spoken. And I, his servant, had to obey.

All around me, the wreaths of aromatic incense swirled and danced like silken veils, glinting in the torchlight as the darkness of the eclipse intensified. The smoke encircled my face, filling my eyes, my mouth and coiling up my nostrils.

Sweet. Sour . . .

As I stood there, the distinctive odour of the incense stirred something deep within me. I breathed in that smell – sweet, yet sour. It reminded me of . . . of . . .

A Stover's pasty!

The juicy smell of the pasty's thick gravy, coupled with the mouthwatering aroma of the syrupy spiced apples, came flooding back to me. And as it did so, a vision of Mei Ling's face floated before me, her forehead wrinkled in a frown and her beautiful eyes full of concern.

'*Cut out his beating heart, slave!*' the skull's voice hissed in my head.

The stone knife trembled in my hands.

'Look into the spaces in the mist . . .' I recalled Mei Ling's melodic voice, so different from that of the ancient skull.

'The mist . . .' I murmured as I stared at the dancing coils of smoke which drifted up from the pots of smouldering incense. As I had done so many times before – in the chamber above the Chinese laundry; in my attic rooms – I found my gaze focusing in on the spaces: those long tunnels which opened up and spiralled away into the distance. I entered the world of what isn't there; the world of silence and stillness and empty spaces—

'*Cut out his beating heart!*' The emerald skull's voice rose to an agitated scream as the heartbeat quickened.

Below me, the schoolboys banged their weapons to the same beat – pounding their clubs and cudgels against the stone pavement of the quad, chanting as they did so.

'Catincatapetl! Catincatapetl!'

I could feel the blood-red eyes of the emerald skull boring into me, together with the black, masked stares of the eleven prefects and the wide, terrified eyes of the head-master. But I kept my gaze on the coiling smoke, Mei Ling's gentle words replacing those of the hideous skull.

'Step into the empty spaces, Barnaby.'

Empty spaces . . .

The art of absence.

The Way of the Silver Mist.

Yinchido.

'*Obey me, slave!*' the head roared.

Its power swirled about me, threatening at any moment to suck me down into a dark whirlpool of oblivion. Instead, with a mighty effort of will, I focused on the glowing light that was Mei Ling and . . .

. . . let go of the stone knife.

It clattered onto the mahogany surface of the desk, before tumbling over the edge and down into the quad below. There was a great collective gasp, followed by a ghastly rattle and chattering of teeth as the emerald skull shook on its cushion with impotent fury.

'*Sacrilege!*' the ancient voice shrieked. '*Destroy him!*'

The prefects turned, advancing towards me, their clubs and cudgels raised. The heartbeat pounded in the eerie darkness as if beating out a rhythm to their attack.

Thud! Thud! Thud!

The tall prefect in the crown of iridescent blue plumage attacked first, swinging a vicious-looking spiked cudgel which, before the nine-inch nails had been hammered in, had once been an innocent piano leg. I focused on the space between the prefect and his swinging arm and stepped into it.

'*Oof!*'

The prefect exhaled, his mask slipping, as

the cudgel sliced through thin air, then lost his balance and toppled from the platform. As he disappeared from view, four more of the prefects took his place.

'*Destroy him!*' the head screamed. '*Destroy him!*'

Two of them swung heavy studded clubs at my head. I ducked down, then sprang immediately backward to avoid a third club. There was a crash as the three clubs struck one another and their owners toppled off the platform and down to the quad below. The fourth prefect – a hefty individual with curly black hair and a great hooked beak strapped to his face – came at me with a long pole, a dagger bound to its end to form a makeshift spear.

As the blade whistled past my left ear, I feinted a movement to the right, before leaping high up into the air to avoid another swinging thrust. The prefect groaned as he too lost his balance. One moment he hovered at the edge of the platform, arms wheeling frantically; the next, with a loud cry of despair, he tumbled back and clattered down the side of the pyramid, to the groans of the schoolboys below.

I turned to face the other prefects. There were six of them remaining, the blood-red light streaming from the skull's ruby eyes throwing them into sinister silhouette. With howls of rage, they charged at me, cudgels, fives bats, mallets and spears swinging.

I stepped into the writhing, weaving spaces between the flurry of blows that rained down, with the slipperiness of a canal otter in a crowded lock. The prefects scattered and fell as their blows caught each other and left me unscathed. With a final nudge in the back, I sent the last of my feather-caped attackers hurtling from the top of the pyramid.

Ignoring the howls of the mob below, I knelt down and picked up a discarded fives bat. I turned and approached the high-backed leather chair. Behind me, I could hear the headmaster's whimpering voice.

'My poor, poor children ... All my fault ... All my fault ...'

In front of me, on its cushion, the emerald skull's eyes flared a brilliant, dazzling white.

'*It is not too late, my child,*' its voice, almost pleading, hissed in my head. '*Not too late, my child. Look into my eyes ...*'

Face buried in the musty emerald-feathered softness of my cape, I reached forward and grasped the skull in one hand.

'*No! No! No!*' it shrieked, as if sensing what was to come.

Bracing myself, legs wide apart and firmly planted on the platform, I tossed the emerald skull high into the air and brought my bat back behind my shoulders. The skull reached the highest point of its trajectory. Then, as it began to descend – the voice screaming and the heartbeat thumping more feverishly

The skull . . . shot off into the darkness.

than ever – I focused on the water butt in the far corner of the quad and, with all my might . . .

Thwack!

The skull made hard contact with the centre of the fives bat and shot off into the darkness.

'*Sacrilege!*' it screamed. '*Sacril—*'

From the far side of the quad there came a loud splash and a steamy hiss as the skull landed in the water butt.

The thud of the heartbeat stopped and, for a moment, nobody breathed in the now silent quad. At that instant the moon completed its passage across the face of the sun and dazzling shafts of light bore down from the sky above. As the eclipse passed, the grounds were once again bathed in warm sunlight. Birds sang. Dogs barked. And in the quad of Grassington Hall the large crowd of boys took in a huge gulp of breath and fell, coughing and spluttering, to their knees.

A moment later, the quad was buzzing with bewildered voices.

'What happened?'

'What's this?'

'What are you wearing?'

From my vantage point at the top of the great pyramid, I looked around. One boy picked up the discarded stone knife and turned it over in his hand. Another pulled off a feathered head-dress and inspected it. A group of three or four helped a dazed prefect to his feet. Some others untied the line of shaken masters. Some wept and clung to one another, fatigue and relief overwhelming them in equal measure ...

The Grassington Hall school rebellion was over.

I turned to the mahogany desk, where the headmaster still lay, bound hand and foot, with the grotesque red cross on his chest.

'It was all my fault, Barnaby,' he whispered tremulously, clutching my hands.

'It wasn't their fault, poor children.'

'It's over, Headmaster,' I said gently, untying him and helping him to his feet. 'The madness is over. No harm done . . .'

I stopped, a painful lump rising in my throat as I suddenly thought of poor Thompson lying in the entrance hall in a pool of his own blood. A watery film over my eyes made the bustling quad blur, and I swallowed hard. Archimedes Barnett must have mistaken my emotion for relief, for he grasped my hands.

'Thanks to you, Barnaby Grimes,' he murmured, squeezing my hands gratefully. 'All thanks to you.'

'One lump or two, Barnaby?'

'Two, please, Headmaster,' I replied.

I glanced out of the window of the head-master's study. It was difficult to believe that, only four short weeks earlier, a massive wooden pyramid had dominated the whole quad. Now it was gone – the broken cabinets and tables used to stoke up the school boilers – and brand-new desks, dining tables, cabi-nets and doors had been brought in to replace them. They were the very finest the city workshops could provide. And I should know; I had just placed the final invoices and work-orders on the headmaster's new mahogany desk.

My new friend, Will Farmer, had helped me with the mass of paperwork that refitting the school had entailed. He was a quick learner and not without talent. The lad would go far.

The headmaster passed me a cup of tea, which I stirred slowly. He ran a finger over the polished surface of his new desk.

'Bit of an extravagance, I know. But I couldn't face the thought of the old one, not after . . .' Archimedes Barnett shuddered.

I nodded and took a sip of the warm sweet tea. I knew how he felt. The sight of poor Thompson will always haunt me. But could I have handled things differently?

'It was all my fault,' said the headmaster. 'If it hadn't been for me and my stupid bird collecting—'

'You mustn't blame yourself, Headmaster,' I said, putting down my cup. 'You might as well blame the archaeologist who dug up the skull in the first place. Or me, for delivering it—'

'You have nothing to reproach yourself for, Barnaby,' said the headmaster hotly. 'Why, if you hadn't been here, I shudder to think what might have happened.'

We were silent for a moment, both lost in thought.

I had a pretty good idea what might have happened. After all, I'd had four weeks to look into it – during late nights spent poring over dusty volumes from the shelves of Underhill's Library for Scholars of the Arcane.

Catincatapetl – Emerald Messenger of Darkness, Master of the Underworld and Lord of Chaos – was at once one of the most feared and one of the most revered gods of an ancient jungle civilization.

Mysterious and mystical, this civilization's ruined cities, with their great stepped pyramids, had drawn archaeologists and treasure hunters over the years, like anteaters to a termite mound. Most came away with little more than a few shards of pottery and a bad case of jungle fever.

The real jewels of the jungle weren't mythical treasures buried beneath ancient ruins at all, but the exotically coloured birds of the forest, with their magnificent plumage.

Collectors like Archimedes Barnett couldn't get enough of such specimens as 'the blue-crested bird of heaven', 'the vermilion hummingbird' or 'the emerald messenger', and were prepared to pay handsomely for them. Supplying exotic birds proved a neat sideline for any enterprising archaeologist.

Professor Rodrigo de Vargas was, from what I gathered in my research, one of the most enterprising. He was an expert on the savage cult of the god Catincatapetl. According to legend, Catincatapetl's followers offered up human sacrifices of such number and with such barbarity that the neighbouring tribes finally rose up in revulsion and destroyed their civilization.

Catincatapetl disappeared into the mists of time, remembered only as a name given to a rare and beautiful bird of the jungle, 'catincatapetl, emerald messenger of darkness'. Until, that is, Professor Rodrigo de Vargas made the discovery of his career, digging in the ruins of a forgotten jungle pyramid.

The fabulous jewel-encrusted skull that he uncovered from beneath a heavy stone slab gazed up at him with glowing eyes of ancient malevolence. De Vargas was the first of a chain of mortals to fall under the skull's evil influence. A year ago, according to newspaper cuttings, Professor de Vargas's treasure hunting came to an abrupt end when his body was found in the gutter in the port of Valdario.

Of course, a jewel-encrusted skull from an ancient civilization would have created a sensation on the international art market, but Catincatapetl had other plans . . .

Not long after, a Captain Luis Fernandez of the SS *Ipanema* offered up for sale a rare specimen of 'the emerald messenger of darkness' to interested bird collectors on the open market. Strangely, although many lucrative offers from bird collectors from that part of the world were not slow in coming, the captain would accept only one – from the headmaster of a private school in a far-off country, for which he set sail. It was a country that, the almanacs revealed, would soon experience a total eclipse of the sun. The hapless captain and his crew were never seen again . . .

The rest, as they say, is history.

We were all pawns in the evil scheming of Catincatapetl as he sought to regain power after untold centuries buried beneath a jungle ruin. But thanks to Mei Ling, and the art of yinchido that she'd so expertly taught me, I had managed to break free from its evil stranglehold for an instant. It was all I'd needed . . .

Finishing my tea, I followed the head-master as he walked me across the quad towards the playing fields.

'I don't suppose,' said Archimedes Barnett, frowning as we approached a discoloured stain in the corner of the quad, 'that you have had any luck tracing our missing water butt?'

I shook my head. In the turmoil and confusion following the solar eclipse, nobody had noticed the two workmen arriving to help with the clear-up. Along with the wrecked desks and cupboards, the water butt had ended up in the back of a cart.

'Disappeared on its travels,' I said grimly. 'Searching for another eclipse . . .'

Archimedes smiled. 'Which, according to my almanac, Barnaby, won't be for another seventy-one years. By which time,' he added with a nod towards the playing fields, 'we should be well and truly prepared for it.'

I looked across the field. There on the pitch was a raised mound, on which eleven boys – fives mallets held high – were attempting to tackle a twelfth, who dodged and dived past them. Reaching the far end of the mound, he grasped a ball the size of a head from a set of wooden stumps, and hurled it with all his might towards a net on the other side of the pitch, while members of his own team cheered from the sideline.

'Green skull!' they cried out as the ball landed in the net.

'What are they playing?' I asked, turning to the headmaster.

'Our new school game,' he replied, beaming back at me. 'We call it "Grimes".'

PAUL & CHRIS
STEWART RIDDELL

LEGION of the DEAD

*Turn the page for an exclusive peek at the
first chapter of the new Barnaby Grimes
book, in stores Winter 2010.*

CHAPTER 1

I have heard people exclaim that they'd be better off dead – weary washerwomen on a midnight shift in the steam cellars, ragged beggars down by the Temple Bar, fine young ladies snubbed at a Hightown ball . . . But if they had seen what I saw on that cold and foggy night, they would have realized the foolishness of their words.

It was a sight that will haunt me till my dying day – after which, I fervently hope and pray, I shall remain undisturbed.

This was not something that could be said for the ghastly apparitions that stumbled through the swirling mists towards me, their arms outstretched before them, as though their bony fingertips rather than their sunken eyes were guiding their lurching bodies through the curdled fog.

A wizened hag, there was, with a hooked nose and rat's nest hair. A portly matron, the ague that had seen her off still glistening on her furrowed brow . . . A sly-eyed ragger and a bare-knuckled wrestler, his left eyeball out of its socket and dangling on a glistening thread. A corpulent costermonger; a stooped scrivener, their clothes – one satin and frill, the other threadbare serge – smeared alike with black mud and sewer slime. A maid, a chimney-sweep, a couple of stable-lads; one with the side of his skull stoved in by a single blow from a horse's hoof, the other grey and glittery-eyed from the blood-flecked cough that had ended his life. And a burly river-tough – his fine waistcoat in tatters and his chin-tattoo obscured by filth. Glistening at his neck was the deep wound that had taken him from this world to the next.

I shrank back in horror and pressed hard against the cool white marble of the de Vere family vault at my back. Beside me – his body quivering like a slab of jellied ham – the Colonel was breathing in stuttering, wheezy gasps. From three sides of the marble tomb in that fog-filled graveyard, the serried ranks of the undead were forming up in a grotesque parody of a parade-ground drill.

'They've found me,' the Colonel croaked, in a voice not much more than a whisper.

I followed his terrified gaze and found myself staring at four ragged figures in military uniform, who were standing on a flat-topped tomb above the massed ranks. Each of them bore the evidence of fatal injuries.

The terrible gash down the face of one that had left his cheekbone exposed and a flap of leathery skin dangling. The blood-stained chest and jagged stump – all that remained of his left arm – of the second, splinters of yellow bone protruding through the wreaths of grimy bandages. The rusting axe, cleaving the battered bell-top shako, which was embedded in the skull of the third. And the bulging bloodshot eyes of the fourth, the frayed length of rough rope that had strangulated his last breath still hanging round his bruised and red-raw neck – and a flagpole clutched in his gnarled hands.

As I watched, he raised the splintered flagpole high. Gripping my swordstick, I stared at the fluttering curtain of blood-stained cloth, tasselled brocade hanging in filthy matted strands along the four sides. At its centre was the embroidered regimental emblem – a snake and a bear – framed in a golden oval, and set off beneath with the words *33rd Regiment of Foot* written in an angular italic script. The ghastly standard-bearer's tight lips parted to reveal a row of blackened teeth.

'Fighting Thirty-Third!' he cried out, his voice a rasping whisper.

The corpses swayed where they stood, their bony arms outstretched before them and tattered sleeves hanging limply in the foggy air. I smelled the sourness of the sewers about them; that, and the sweet whiff of death. Their sunken eyes bored into mine.

We were surrounded. There was nothing Colonel de Vere or I could do. The standard-bearer's voice echoed hoarsely round the graveyard.

'Advance!'

Watch out for

LEGION OF THE DEAD

in Winter 2010.

THE EDGE CHRONICLES

THE QUINT TRILOGY

Follow the adventures of Quint
in the first age of flight!

CURSE OF THE GLOAMGLOZER

Quint and Maris, daughter of the most High
Academe, are plunged into a terrifying adventure
which takes them deep into the rock upon which
Sanctaphrax is built. Here they unwittingly invoke
an ancient curse . . .

THE WINTER KNIGHTS

Quint is a new student at the Knights Academy,
struggling to survive the icy cold of a never-ending
winter, and the ancient feuds that threaten
Sanctaphrax.

CLASH OF THE SKY GALLEONS

Quint finds himself caught up in his father's fight
for revenge against the man who killed his family.
They are drawn into a deadly pursuit, a pursuit that
will ultimately lead to the clash of the great
sky galleons.

'The most amazing books ever'
Ellen, **10**

THE EDGE CHRONICLES

THE TWIG TRILOGY

*Follow the adventures of Twig
in the first age of flight!*

BEYOND THE DEEPWOODS

Abandoned at birth in the perilous Deepwoods,
Twig does what he has always been warned not to
do, and strays from the path . . .

STORMCHASER

Twig, a young crew-member on the Stormchaser
sky ship, risks all to collect valuable stormphrax
from the heart of a Great Storm.

MIDNIGHT OVER SANCTAPHRAX

Far out in Open Sky, a ferocious storm is brewing.
In its path is the city of Sanctaphrax . . .

'Absolutely brilliant'
Lin-May, **13**

**'Everything about the Edge
Chronicles is amazing'**
Cameron, **13**

THE EDGE CHRONICLES

THE ROOK TRILOGY

*Follow the adventures of Rook
in the second age of flight!*

LAST OF THE SKY PIRATES

Rook dreams of becoming a librarian knight,
and sets out on a dangerous journey into the
Deepwoods and beyond. When he meets the last sky
pirate, he is thrust into a bold adventure . . .

VOX

Rook becomes involved in the evil scheming of
Vox Verlix – can he stop the Edgeworld falling into
total chaos?

FREEGLADER

Undertown is destroyed, and Rook and his
friends travel, with waifs and cloddertrogs, to a new
home in the Free Glades.

'They're the best!!' *Zaffie*, 15

'Brilliant illustrations and magical storylines'
Tom, 14

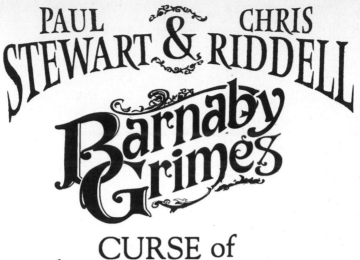

CURSE of
the NIGHT WOLF

Barnaby Grimes is a tick-tock lad – he'll deliver any message anywhere any time. As fast as possible. Tick-tock – time is money! But strange things are afoot. One moonlit night, as Barnaby highstacks above the city, leaping from roof to roof, gutter to gable, pillar to pediment, a huge beast attacks. He barely escapes with his life. And now his friend Old Benjamin has disappeared . . .

A gloriously macabre tale in a breathtaking new series, packed with intrigue, horror and fantastic illustrations. From the creators of the bestselling Edge Chronicles.

'A page-turning adventure, written with gusto and inventiveness' SUNDAY TIMES

Visit **www.stewartandriddell.co.uk**
for all you need to know about Barnaby Grimes,
the Edge Chronicles and Far-Flung Adventures.
With games, secret areas, maps, characters, and
a regular diary from the authors.